MW01277110

## ORACIONES PARA NIÑOS Y NIÑAS

PRESENTADO A

_____

FECHA

_____

POR

_____

# Precious® Moments

## ORACIONES PARA NIÑOS Y NIÑAS

Ilustraciones por
SAM BUTCHER
Oraciones por
DEBBIE BUTCHER WIERSMA

BETANIA

Betania es un sello de Editorial Caribe, Inc.

© 2003 Editorial Caribe, Inc.
Una división de Thomas Nelson, Inc.
Nashville, TN—Miami, FL, EE.UU.
www.caribebetania.com

Título en inglés: Prayers for Boys & Girls
© 1990, 1997, 2003 Precious Moments, Inc.
Publicado por Word Publishing
una división de Thomas Nelson, Inc.

Arte © 2003 Precious Moments, Inc.
Concesionario: Editorial Caribe/Thomas Nelson Bible

Traductor: Eugenio Orellana

A menos que se señale lo contrario, las citas bíblicas han sido tomada
de la Versión en Lenguaje Sencillo, © 2000 Sociedad Bíblicas Unidas. También
se han utilizado las siguientes tres versiones: La Biblia al Día (LBD),
© 1973 Living Bible International;  la Biblia Dios Habla Hoy (DHH),
© Sociedad Bíblicas Unidas 1966, 1970, 1979, 1983, 1996; y la
Reina-Valera Revisada, © 1960 Sociedades Bíblicas en América Latina.
Usadas con permiso.

ISBN: 0-88113-723-5

Impreso en Colombia
Printed in Colombia

# CONTENIDO

Nota a los padres  6

# NOTA A LOS PADRES

Instruye al niño en su camino,
Y aun cuando fuere viejo
no se apartará de él.

PROVERBIOS 22.6 RVR 1960

Jesús dijo: «Dejen a los niños que vengan a mí...»

En estas páginas encontrarán veinte oraciones, escritas específicamente para niños. Para hablar con Dios, los niños usan un lenguaje sencillo, directo y sincero. Estas oraciones, por lo tanto, son sencillas, directas y además, sinceras.

Es nuestra esperanza que los padres lean estas oraciones en voz alta a sus hijos y que estos se sientan animados a expresar libremente lo que piensan y lo que sienten.

También es nuestra esperanza que estas oraciones lleguen a ser modelos que los niños puedan usar para crear sus propias oraciones.

# GRACIAS, SEÑOR

Den gracias al Señor,
porque él es bueno,
porque su amor es eterno.

1 Crónicas 16.34 DHH

# POR MI CUERPO
# Y POR MI MENTE

Me gusta como me hiciste, Señor.

Me alegro que me diste piernas y brazos y pies y dedos en las manos y en los pies. Que tenga ojos y oídos y una nariz y una boca y muchos dientes.

Tengo todo lo que necesito para gozarme en el mundo que hiciste. Puedo hacer muchas cosas con el cuerpo que me diste. Puedo ir a donde quiero y hacer lo que desee.

Pero lo mejor en cuanto a mí es que tengo una mente para pensar y aprender de ti.

Gracias, Señor, por hacerme como soy.

Amén.

Soy una creación maravillosa,
y por eso te doy gracias.
SALMOS 139.14

# POR MI AMIGO CUANDO VOY A DORMIR

Gracias, Señor, por mi querido amigo cuando me voy a dormir.

Qué lindo es sentir sus orejas, tan suaves y velludas. No me da miedo cuando mi cuarto está oscuro porque tengo a mi amigo. A veces, cuando me siento triste, hundo mi rostro en su panza y lloro. Él me hace sentir mejor. Ha sido mi amigo por tanto tiempo que no sé si alguna vez he vivido sin él.

Gracias por darme un amigo tan especial.

Amén.

Él es bueno y nos
da todo lo que necesitamos
para que lo disfrutemos
1 Timoteo 6.17

# POR LOS PAJARITOS

Gracias, Señor, por hacer los pajaritos.
Me gusta verlos volar para arriba, para abajo y hacer
piruetas en el aire. Cuando remontan el cielo, pienso
en los ángeles. Lo mejor de los pajaritos es su canto.
Gracias, Señor, por los pájaros que cantan para mí.
Amén.

Que haya también aves
que vuelen sobre la tierra.
GÉNESIS 1.20 DHH

# POR MIS AMIGOS

Mis amigos son muy importantes para mí.

Me hacen reír cuando no me siento bien. Salen conmigo y juegan los juegos que a mí me gustan. Yo puedo confiar en que ellos guardarán todos mis secretos. Cuando estamos juntos siempre lo pasamos muy bien.

Gracias por darme amigos tan buenos.

Amén.

Yo amo a los que me aman.

PROVERBIOS 8.17 DHH

# POR LA LLUVIA

Gracias, Señor, por la lluvia. A veces cuando llueve me
siento triste porque no puedo salir afuera a jugar.
Luego pienso en todas las cosas buenas que produce la
lluvia. La lluvia riega las flores y el césped en mi patio.
La lluvia da de beber a los árboles. La lluvia riega las
siembras de los agricultores. Cuando pienso en todas
estas cosas buenas de la lluvia, me siento feliz en lugar
de estar triste. Oh, casi olvidaba la mejor parte de la
lluvia: hace el barro para que chapoteemos en él.
Gracias, Señor, por hacer que llueva.
Amén.

Dios cubre de nubes el cielo. Dios hace llover sobre la tierra.

SALMOS 147.8

# POR MI MASCOTA

Gracias, querido Señor, por mi mascota. Algunos de mis amigos tienen perros y gatos. Otros tienen peces y pajarillos. Hay hasta quienes tienen serpientes y lagartos como mascotas. Mi mascota es lo perfecto para mí. Puedo cuidarla y quererla, e incluso puedo saber cuánto me quiere. Cuando tengo el peor día de mi vida, llego a casa y veo a mi mascota haciendo algo divertido y en seguida todos mis malestares desaparecen. Se me dibuja una sonrisa en el rostro. Quiero darte las gracias por mi mascota.
Amén.

¡Hombres y animales están bajo tu cuidado.
SALMOS 36.6

# POR MI FAMILIA

Gracias, Señor, por mi familia.

Yo creo que tengo la mejor familia del mundo.

A veces nos disgustamos y a veces discutimos. Pero yo siempre sé que mi familia me ama.

Nos ayudamos con nuestros problemas, y mi familia siempre parece entender cuando me siento triste. He tenido muchos días hermosos con mi familia. Siempre que estoy con ellos me siento feliz.

Señor, me siento muy contento que hayas decidido darme esta familia para que fuera mi familia.

Amén.

Con sabiduría se construye la casa.

PROVERBIOS 24.3 DHH

# LO SIENTO, SEÑOR

Eres un Dios
de perdón,
siempre dispuesto
a perdonar

NEHEMÍAS 9.17 DHH

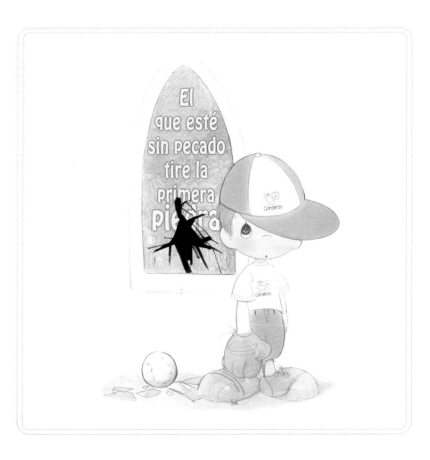

# SOBRE MENTIR

Hoy dije una mentira, Señor.

No era una mentira grande. No creí que fuera a causarle daño a nadie por decir una mentira. Pero lo causé, Señor. Me hizo sufrir saber que había mentido. Aunque nadie llegara a saberlo nunca, yo lo sé.

Señor, ayúdame para que de aquí en adelante no vuelva a mentir. Y que cuando quiera decir una mentira, tú me recuerdes lo mal que me voy a sentir después. Quiero decir siempre la verdad para que los demás siempre me crean.

Perdóname, Señor, por mentir.

Amén.

Apártate de la mentira.
PROVERBIOS 4.24 DHH

# SOBRE HACER FRAUDE

Querido Señor, por favor perdóname por lo que hice hoy día.

Hice fraude en un examen en la escuela. No sabía la respuesta. No quería sacarme una mala nota, de modo que copié la respuesta de mi compañero.

Sé que hacer fraude es malo, pero en ese momento no se me ocurrió pensar que era malo. Tendré que decirle a la profesora lo que hice, pero necesito que me ayudes a decírselo.

Por favor, ayúdame a decir la verdad y a nunca más hacer fraude.

Amén.

Sabes todo lo que hago.

SALMOS 139.3 DHH

# SOBRE PELEAR

Hoy peleé con alguien, Señor.

Aunque yo dije que la culpa había sido del otro, y este dijo que la culpa había sido mía, ambos nos echamos la culpa. Si no hubiéramos querido, no habríamos peleado. ¡Pero estábamos tan furiosos!

A mí, Señor, no me gusta pelear. No es peleando como se arreglan las cosas. Me gustaría ser lo suficientemente inteligente como para hablar con alguien sobre un problema en lugar de acudir a los golpes.

Siento haber golpeado a aquel niño, Señor.

Amén.

El necio da rienda suelta a sus impulsos.
PROVERBIOS 29.11 DHH

# SOBRE HERIR LOS SENTIMIENTOS DE LOS DEMÁS

Me siento mal por lo que hice hoy, Señor.
Dije algo muy feo a mi amigo, y eso hirió sus
sentimientos. Parecía que iba a llorar. Yo quise recoger
las palabras que había dicho, pero ya era demasiado
tarde.
Me siento horrible. Tendré que decirle cuánto lo siento
porque si no, me sentiré peor. Ayúdale a que me
perdone. Y en cuanto a mí, ayúdame a pensar antes de
decir una barbaridad.
En tu nombre oro.
Amén.

Hay quienes hieren con sus palabras.
PROVERBIOS 12.18 DHH

# AYÚDAME, SEÑOR

Dios siempre nos ayuda
cuando estamos en problemas..

Salmos 46.1

# CUANDO ESTOY ABURRIDO

Querido Señor, hoy necesito que me ayudes.
Está lloviendo y afuera está todo mojado y no se me ocurre nada. No quiero jugar con mis juguetes. No quiero leer mis libros. Tampoco quiero jugar con mi mascota.
Ayúdame a pensar en algo divertido que hacer.
Gracias, Señor.
Amén

No sabes lo que
el mañana traerá.
PROVERBIOS 27.1 DHH

# CUANDO TENGA MIEDO

Señor, ayúdame a no tener miedo.

Cuando por las noches me voy a acostar está tan oscuro. Todo parece diferente a como lo veo en el día. Mi ventana se ve terrible cuando a través de ella pasa la luz de la calle. Las sombras oscuras están por todo mi cuarto. Todo está tan silencioso.

Es como si allí no viviera nadie más que yo. Yo sé que tú siempre estás conmigo, Señor, y que no tengo que tenerle miedo a nada. Pero de todos modos, cuando está tan oscuro y silencioso, me da miedo.

Ayúdame a recordar que tú, Señor, estás siempre cerca de mí, incluso en las noches más oscuras. Gracias. Amén.

No tendré miedo, porque
tú irás siempre muy junto a mí.
SALMOS 23.4 LBD

# CUANDO ALGUIEN NO ES SIMPÁTICO

Un compañerito en la escuela es realmente peleador, Señor.

Siempre me está molestando y provocando.

A veces me amedrenta. Otras veces me dice cosas desagradables. Sus palabras me hieren, Señor. Cuando me habla así, me dan ganas de llorar.

Cuando pienso en él me siento mal. Me dan ganas de golpearlo, pero no puedo porque sé que hacer tal cosa es malo.

Ayúdame a encontrar la manera de alejarme de él. Y, Señor, si él quisiera molestarme conmigo, dame fuerzas para soportarlo.

Amén

Sonríe
Dios te
ama

El Señor protege a los
que en él confían.
PROVERBIOS 30.5 DHH

# AYUDA A OTROS, SEÑOR

Tú cuidas de
quienes te respetan
y confían en tu amor.

SALMOS 33.18

# POR LOS NIÑOS QUE ESTÁN HAMBRIENTOS

Querido Señor, algunos niños se irán a la cama esta noche con hambre, y yo quiero orar por ellos.

Algunos niños nunca han sentido la barriga satisfecha.

No tienen las vitaminas que necesitan por lo que no pueden crecer fuertes y saludables. Sus padres no tienen suficiente dinero para comprar la comida que necesitan.

Yo soy muy feliz al tener lo que tengo, oh Dios, pero quisiera orar por esos otros niños. Ayúdales a tener una vida mejor.

Amén

Dichoso el generoso, el que
da de comer a los pobres.
PROVERBIOS 22.9 LBD

# POR LOS ANCIANOS

Querido Señor, cuida a los ancianos del mundo.

Los ancianos han tenido años de experiencia; sin embargo, pareciera que nadie se interesara por ellos. Debe ser terrible sentirse solo, Señor. Algunos ancianos tienen hijos, nietos e incluso bisnietos, pero pocos van a visitarlos.

Yo quiero hacer algo para ayudarles. Puedo preparar y llevarles galletas a los ancianos de mi barrio o ayudarles a comprar sus cosas en el almacén de víveres. Pero más importante que todo eso, puedo visitarles y oír las historias que me quieran contar.

Amén

Todos deben estar dispuestos a escuchar a los demás.

Santiago 1.19

# POR LOS POLICÍAS Y BOMBEROS

Señor, quisiera orar por los policías y los bomberos. Ellos se arriesgan por ayudar a personas que jamás han visto. Los bomberos entran en los edificios en llamas para salvar a alguien que pudiera estar atrapado. Los policías tratan de dar cuidarnos a todos haciendo que obedezcan las reglas y las leyes.

Cuida de los policías y de los bomberos que cuidan tan bien de mí. Gracias, Señor.

Amén

Cuando hay tribulación, él es el mejor refugio.
NAHÚM 1.7 LBD

# POR LAS PERSONAS QUE NO TIENEN CASA

Señor, ayuda a la gente en todo el mundo que no tiene
una casa donde vivir.

Yo tengo un lugar agradable y seguro, pero hay quienes
no lo tienen. Viven en edificios viejos y derruidos.
Algunos de ellos viven en las calles.

Por favor, ayuda a estas personas a encontrar una
verdadera casa y una cama suave donde dormir.

Gracias, Señor.

Amén

Nunca niegues un favor a quien te lo pida.
PROVERBIOS 3.27 DHH

# POR MAMÁ Y PAPÁ

Querido Señor, ser padres debe ser realmente difícil. Tienen que trabajar para ganar dinero para sostener a la familia. Hay que mantener la casa limpia y cocinar. A veces, al final del día, mamá y papá se ven cansados. Por favor, cuídalos. Gracias, Señor.

Honra a tu padre y a tu madre.
ÉXODO 20.12

# Hail
## to the
# Chief

*By Jim McMullan*

General Publishing Group  Los Angeles

*Publisher:* W. Quay Hays
*Managing Editor:* Colby Allerton
*Art Directors:* Interior, Phillis Stacy; Jacket, Susan Anson
*Production Director:* Nadeen Torio
*Projects Manager:* Trudihope Schlomowitz

Cover photo and presidential photo montage courtesy of
the collections of The Library of Congress

For information:
General Publishing Group
2701 Ocean Park Boulevard, Suite 140
Santa Monica, CA 90405

©1996 by Jim McMullan

Library of Congress Catalog Card Number: 96-076635
ISBN: 1-881649-85-7

Printed in the USA
10 9 8 7 6 5 4 3 2 1

General Publishing Group
*Los Angeles*

# *Introduction*

*F*orty one Presidents have come and gone. Their deeds and words are history now...Their countless speeches and eloquent statements have amused, angered and encouraged us and we are all the better for their imagination and inspiration.

Many of our Presidents were poets who, with a phrase, could motivate a nation into action...Some touched our hearts and changed our lives...

Abraham Lincoln, in his Gettysburg Address, told us that "Fourscore and seven years ago our fathers brought forth on this continent, a new nation, conceived in liberty, and dedicated to the proposition that all men are created equal"—he helped to free the slaves.

When Franklin D. Roosevelt, during a great time of stress for America, inspired us with, "The only thing we have to fear is fear itself," he reached out and soothed a worried nation...and...

When John F. Kennedy told us to "Ask not what your country can do for you, but ask what you can do for your country," he triggered a spark of hope in us, and we responded by giving him our best.

Some Presidents were more articulate than others; some had very little to say…In this book you will encounter the thoughts and insights by those who had much to say…Some were clever and funny, some were serious and businesslike, others inspired us with their vision and some just simply annoyed us.

This collection was two hundred years in the making. It started way back in 1789, when George Washington became our first President and it continues with the words of Bill Clinton…Two hundred years of colorful history…Two Hundred years of erudition…Two hundred years and 42 Presidents later, we look back and remember the pleasure, the pain, and the drama that helped establish this magnificent country of ours.

I hope the choices I've made will contribute to your pleasure. I had a delightful time pursuing them. If some don't please you, I can only refer you to something Franklin D. Roosevelt said in 1944… "I have no expectation of making a hit every time I come to bat."

—*Jim McMullan*

# Acknowledgments

*I gratefully acknowledge the assistance of the following:*

To everyone at General Publishing Group.

To Quay Hays, president of General Publishing Group, who shared my vision to bring this book to fruition.

To Colby Allerton, my hard-working editor, who diligently pressed forward to deliver the book on time.

To Peter Hoffman, my second talented editor at GPG.

To Eleanor Neumaier for her last minute proofread.

*A special thanks to the following archivists who went out of their way to be of help:*

Dwight M. Miller - Herbert Hoover Library
James W. Leyerzapf - Dwight D. Eisenhower Library
Samuel W. Rushay - Harry S. Truman Library
Linda Hanson and Mike Parrish - Lyndon Baines Johnson Library
Bert Nason - Jimmy Carter Library
Jennifer A. Sternaman - Gerald R. Ford Library

*And to:*
Gabrielle Bushman and Russell Horwitz at the the White House speech writing and research department.

To my dad, Jim McMullan Sr., the political voice of our family, who encouraged me to pay heed to presidential utterances.

To my wife, Helene, and my boys, Sky & Tysun, for their ongoing good thoughts and inspiration.

To Mrs. Kelly, my fifth-grade teacher at Central School in Long Beach, NY, who told me that I could be President someday if I worked hard.

And last but not least…A generous thank you, with drum rolls, bugle blasts and a walloping fanfare to all the Presidents past and present whose glorious words fill this book…I couldn't have done it without them.

1 George Washington (1732-1799)
   *President from: 1789 to 1797*

2 John Adams (1735-1826)
   *President from: 1797 to 1801*

3 Thomas Jefferson (1743-1826)
   *President from: 1801 to 1809*

4 James Madison (1751-1836)
   *President from: 1809 to 1817*

5 James Monroe (1758-1831)
   *President from: 1817 to 1825*

6 John Quincy Adams (1767-1848)
   *President from: 1825 to 1829*

7 Andrew Jackson (1767-1845)
   *President from: 1829 to 1837*

8 Martin Van Buren (1782-1862)
   *President from: 1837 to 1841*

9 William Henry Harrison (1773-1841)
   *President in: 1841*

10 John Tyler (1790-1862)
   *President from: 1841 to 1845*

11 James K. Polk (1795-1849)
   *President from: 1845 to 1849*

12 Zachary Taylor (1784-1850)
   *President from: 1849 to 1850*

13 Millard Fillmore (1800-1874)
   *President from: 1850 to 1853*

14 Franklin Pierce (1804-1869)
   *President from: 1853 to 1857*

15 James Buchanan (1791-1868)
*President from: 1857 to 1861*

16 Abraham Lincoln (1809-1865)
*President from: 1861 to 1865*

17 Andrew Johnson (1808-1875)
*President from: 1865 to 1869*

18 Ulysses S. Grant (1822-1885)
*President from: 1869 to 1877*

19 Rutherford B. Hayes (1822-1893)
*President from: 1877 to 1881*

20  James A. Garfield (1831-1881)
*President in: 1881*

21 Chester A. Arthur (1829-1886)
*President from: 1881 to 1885*

22 Grover Cleveland (1837-1908)
*President from: 1885 to 1889*

23 Benjamin Harrison  (1833-1901)
*President from: 1889 to 1893*

24 Grover Cleveland  (1837-1908)
*President from: 1893 to 1897*

25 William McKinley (1843-1901)
*President from: 1897 to 1901*

26 Theodore Roosevelt (1858-1919)
*President from: 1901 to 1909*

27 William Howard Taft (1857-1930)
*President from: 1909 to 1913*

28 Woodrow Wilson (1856-1924)
*President from: 1913 to 1921*

29 Warren G. Harding (1865-1923)
*President from: 1921 to 1923*

30 Calvin Coolidge (1872-1933)
*President from: 1923 to 1929*

31 Herbert Hoover (1874 -1964 )
*President from: 1929 to 1933*

32 Franklin D. Roosevelt (1882-1945)
*President from: 1933 to 1945*

33 Harry S. Truman (1884-1972)
*President from: 1945 to 1953*

34 Dwight D. Eisenhower (1890-1969)
*President from: 1953 to 1961*

35 John F. Kennedy (1917-1963)
*President from: 1961 to 1963*

36 Lyndon B. Johnson (1908-1973)
*President from: 1963 to 1969*

37 Richard M. Nixon (1913-1994)
*President from: 1969 to 1974*

38 Gerald Ford (1913-   )
*President from: 1974 to 1977*

39 Jimmy Carter (1924-   )
*President from: 1977 to 1981*

4 0 Ronald Reagan (1911-   )
*President from: 1981 to 1989*

41 George Bush (1924-   )
*President from: 1989 to 1993*

42 Bill Clinton (1946-   )
*President from: 1993 to -*

# Table Of Contents

# Democracy and Nationalism

## Part One

We will do the wisest thing of all—we will turn to the only resource we have that in times of need always grows: the goodness and the courage of the American people.

*George Bush*

—••—

I have felt in the last several months that we often get so caught up in the battle of the moment that sometimes we forget that we are all in this because we are seeking a good that helps all Americans. There must be some sense of common purpose and common strength.

*Bill Clinton*

—••—

Knowledge will forever govern ignorance; and a people who mean to be their own governors must arm themselves with the power which knowledge gives.

*James Madison*

—••—

Union, justice, tranquility, the common defense, the general welfare, and the blessings of liberty—all have been promoted by the government under which we have lived. Standing at this point in time, looking back to that generation which has gone by and forward to that which is advancing, we may at once indulge in grateful exultation and in cheering hope.

*John Quincy Adams*

I seek the Presidency for a single purpose...to build a better America.

*George Bush*

---

The founder of this country proclaimed to all the world the revolutionary doctrine of the divine rights of the common man, and that doctrine has ever since been the heart of the American faith.

*Dwight D. Eisenhower*

---

America did not invent human rights. In a very real sense, human rights invented America.

*Jimmy Carter*

---

Unswerving loyalty to duty, constant devotion to truth, and a clear conscience will overcome every discouragement and surely lead the way to usefulness of high achievement.

*Grover Cleveland*

---

When our Founders boldly declared America's independence to the world and our purposes to the Almighty, they knew that America to endure would have to change; not change for change's sake, but change to preserve America's ideals: liberty, the pursuit of happiness.

*Bill Clinton*

The men who mine coal and fire furnaces and balance ledgers and turn lathes and pick cotton and heal the sick and plant corn—all serve America as proudly, and as profitably, as the statesmen who draft treaties and the legislators who enact the laws.

*Dwight D. Eisenhower*

---

Stabilize America first, prosper America first, think of America first and exalt America first.

*Warren G. Harding*

---

I do not know whether it is prejudice or not, but I always have a very high opinion of a state whose chief product is corn.

*Benjamin Harrison*

---

Democracy is a superior form of government because it is based on a respect for man as a reasonable being.

*John F. Kennedy*

---

The meaning of our word "America" flows from one pure source. Within the soul of America is freedom of mind and spirit in man. Here alone are the open windows through which pours the sunlight of the human spirit. Here alone is human dignity not a dream, but an accomplishment.

*Herbert Hoover*

The best form of government is that which is most likely to prevent the greatest sum of evil.

*James Monroe*

---

Government must learn to take less from the people so that people can do more for themselves.

*Richard M. Nixon*

---

Patriotism means looking out for yourself by looking out for your country.

*Calvin Coolidge*

---

It is time to break the habit of expecting something for nothing, from our government or from each other. Let us all take more responsibility for our communities and our country.

*Bill Clinton*

---

In isolation from nature lies the danger of man's isolation from his fellow and from his Creator.

*Lyndon B. Johnson*

---

And so my fellow Americans, ask not what your country can do for you, ask what you can do for your country.

*John F. Kennedy*

Minorities have a right to appeal to the Constitution as a shield against oppression.

*James K. Polk*

———•———

Double...no triple...our troubles and we'll still be better off than any other people on earth.

*Ronald Reagan*

———•———

I have no desire to crow over anybody or to see anybody eating crow, figuratively or otherwise. We should all get together and make a country in which everybody can eat turkey whenever he pleases.

*Harry S. Truman*

———•———

National honor is national property of the highest value.

*James Monroe*

———•———

Let us reject the narrow visions of those who would tell us that we are evil because we are not yet perfect...that all the sweat and toil and sacrifice that have gone into the building of America were for naught because the building is not yet done. Let us see that the path we are traveling is wide, with room in it for all of us, and that its direction is toward a better nation in a more peaceful world.

*Richard M. Nixon*

———•———

America is not a nation in decline. America is a rising nation.

*George Bush*

———•———

We must be willing, individually and as a nation, to accept whatever sacrifices may be required of us. A people who value its privileges above its principles soon lose both.

*Dwight D. Eisenhower*

———•———

The basis of our political system is the right of the people to make and to alter their constitutions of government.

*George Washington*

———•———

If you go into any classroom in America you see the infinite promise of our country in a beautiful essay or a difficult math problem solved, or just an act of kindness from one child to another. And you come face to face with the terrible challenges confronting this country, in children who are old beyond their years because of what they've had to endure, too tired or hurt or closed off from each other and the world to learn.

*Bill Clinton*

———•———

The fate of America cannot depend on any one man. The greatness of America is grounded in principles and not on any single personality.

*Franklin D. Roosevelt*

———•———

Democracy & Nationalism

The second day of July, 1776, will be the most memorable day in the history of America. I am apt to believe that it will be celebrated by succeeding generations as a great anniversary festival. It ought to be commemorated as the day of deliverance, by solemn acts of devotion to God Almighty, pomp and parade, with shows, games, sports, guns, bonfires, and illuminations, from one end of this continent to the other, from this time forward forevermore.

*John Adams*

———

With public sentiment, nothing can fail; without it, nothing can succeed.

*Abraham Lincoln*

———

Only Americans can hurt America.

*Dwight D. Eisenhower*

———

America today is a proud, free nation, decent and civil—a place we cannot help but love. We know in our hearts, not loudly and proudly, but as a simple fact, that this country has meaning beyond what we see, and that our strength is a force for good.

*George Bush*

———

The ballot box is the surest arbiter of disputes among free men.

*James Buchanan*

Let us remember always that finding common ground as we move toward this century depends fundamentally on our shared commitment to equal opportunity for all Americans. It is a moral imperative, a constitutional mandate, and a legal necessity.

*Bill Clinton*

Without organized political parties striving to serve the best interests of the American people, we would descend into political anarchy and be torn into political factions representing selfish, sectional, and group minorities. The purpose of party organization must be to promote the national welfare. Nothing is more certain than that good government is good politics.

*Herbert Hoover*

All free governments are managed by the combined wisdom and folly of the people.

*James A. Garfield*

A voter without a ballot is like a soldier without a bullet.

*Dwight D. Eisenhower*

Great is the stake in our hands; great is the responsibility which must rest upon the people of the United States. Let us realize the importance of the attitude in which we stand before the world. Let us exercise forbearance and firmness. Let us extricate our country from the dangers which surround it and learn wisdom from the lessons they inculcate.

*Andrew Jackson*

---

To be courageous requires no exceptional qualifications, no magic formula, no special combination of time, place and circumstance. It is an opportunity that sooner or later is presented to us all.

*John F. Kennedy*

---

As I would not be a slave, so I would not be a master. This expresses my idea of democracy. Whatever differs from this to the extent of the difference is no democracy.

*Abraham Lincoln*

---

The final battle against intolerance is to be fought—not in the chambers of any legislature—but in the hearts of men.

*Dwight D. Eisenhower*

---

The people of this continent alone have the right to decide their own destiny.

*James K. Polk*

The government of the United States is a limited government. It is confined to the exercise of powers expressly granted and it is at all times an especial duty to guard against any infringement on the just rights of the States.

*Millard Fillmore*

As our 200th anniversary approaches, we owe it to ourselves and to posterity to rebuild our political and economic strength. Let us make America again, and for centuries more to come, what it has so long been—a stronghold and a beacon light of liberty for the whole world.

*Gerald Ford*

Of all the great interests which appertain to our country, the union—cordial, confiding, fraternal union—is by far the most important, since it is the only true and sure guaranty of all the others.

*William Henry Harrison*

The New Frontier of which I speak is not a set of promises—it is a set of challenges. It sums up not what I intend to offer the American people, but what I intend to ask of them.

*John F. Kennedy*

Whatever you are, be a good one.

*Abraham Lincoln*

HE DID NOT SAY THIS!

Our founders wisely selected as our motto, *e pluribus unum*, out of many, one. And Lincoln said that "A house divided against itself cannot stand." Let us build an American home for this century, where everyone has a place at the table, and not a single child is left behind. In this world and the world of tomorrow, we must go forward together or not at all.

*Bill Clinton*

There is no Negro problem. There is no Southern problem. There is no Northern problem. There is only an American problem.

*Lyndon B. Johnson*

Always vote for a principle, though you vote alone, and you will cherish the sweet reflection that your vote is never lost.

*John Quincy Adams*

To all our means of culture is added the powerful incentive to personal ambition. No post of honor is so high but the poorest may hope to reach it.

*James A. Garfield*

Whatever there is of greatness in the United States is due to labor. The laborer is the author of all greatness and wealth. Without labor there would be no government and no leading class.

*Ulysses S. Grant*

The Great Society is not a safe harbor, a resting place, a final objective, a finished work. It is a challenge constantly renewed, beckoning us toward a destiny where the meaning of our lives matches the marvelous products of our labor.

*Lyndon B. Johnson*

---

We must have a citizenship less concerned about what the government can do for it and more anxious about what it can do for the nation.

*Warren G. Harding*

---

In our national community we're all different, we're all the same. We want liberty and freedom. We want the embrace of family and community. We want to make the most of our own lives and we're determined to give our children a better one. Remember we're still closing the gap between our founders' ideals and our reality. But every step has made us richer, stronger, and better.

*Bill Clinton*

---

The delicate duty of devising schemes of revenue should be left where the Constitution placed it—with the representatives of the people.

*William Henry Harrison*

No other people have a government more worthy of their respect and love or a land so magnificent in extent, so pleasant to look upon, and so full of generous suggestion to enterprise and labor. God has placed upon our head a diadem and has laid at our feet power and wealth beyond definition and calculation. But we must not forget that we take these gifts upon the condition that justice and mercy shall hold the reigns of power and that the upward avenues of hope shall be free to all the people.

*Benjamin Harrison*

---

I did not take the sacred oath of office to preside over the decline and fall of the United States of America.

*Gerald Ford*

---

To preserve the American Dream in our time and for your future our leaders must ask tough questions and give strong answers. But people must rally to the cause of change with faith. We have to believe again. We must believe through the smallness and the spite that conflict always brings out in all of us. We must believe through that to the spirit and generosity and courage that is America at its essence.

*Bill Clinton*

---

There is one choice we cannot make. We will not choose the path of submission. The world must be made safe for democracy.

*Woodrow Wilson*

The truly American sentiment recognizes the dignity of labor and the fact that honor lies in honest toil.

*Grover Cleveland*

———

No nation or individual has been able to squander itself into prosperity.

*Herbert Hoover*

———

It is not promulgating anything that I have not heretofore said that traitors must be made odious, that treason must be made odious, that traitors must be punished and impoverished.

*Andrew Johnson*

———

I'm going to build the kind of a nation that President Roosevelt hoped for, President Truman worked for, and President Kennedy died for.

*Lyndon B. Johnson*

———

We need to respect our differences and hear them, but it means, instead of having shrill voices of discord, we need a chorus of harmony. In a chorus of harmony you know there are lots of differences, but you can hear all the voices.

*Bill Clinton*

———

It is no part of America's dream that we should erect a house of material well-being in the cheerless atmosphere of physical blight. Our people will be denied their heritage if they must live out their lives among polluted rivers, spoiled fields and forests, and streets where nothing pleases the eye.

*Lyndon B. Johnson*

If we cannot end now our differences, at least we can help make the world safe for diversity.

*John F. Kennedy*

Mankind, when left to themselves, are unfit for their own government.

*George Washington*

We are citizens of the world; and the tragedy of our times is that we do not know it.

*Woodrow Wilson*

It is alleged that in many communities Negro citizens are practically denied the freedom of the ballot. It is a crime which, if persisted in, will destroy the government itself.

*James A. Garfield*

A society is not a collection of people pursuing their individual, economic, and material self interests. It is a collection of people who believe that by working together they can raise better children, have stronger families, have more meaningful lives, and have something to pass onto the generation that comes behind.

*Bill Clinton*

---

I have never regarded the office of Chief Magistrate as conferring upon the incumbent the power of master over the popular will, but as granting him the power to execute the properly expressed will of the people and not resist it.

*William Henry Harrison*

---

I've always loved my wife, I've always loved my children, I've always loved my grandchildren, and I've always loved my country.

*Dwight D. Eisenhower*

---

The advice nearest to my heart and deepest in my convictions is that the Union of the states be cherished and perpetuated.

*James Madison*

---

Democracy is not a fragile flower but it still needs cultivating.

*Ronald Reagan*

There is every reason to believe that our system of government will soon attain the highest degree of perfection of which human institutions are capable.

*James Monroe*

---

I have spoken of a thousand points of light—of all the community organizations that are spread like stars throughout the nation, doing good.

The old ideas are new again because they are not old, they are timeless: duty, sacrifice, commitment, and a patriotism that finds its expression in taking part and pitching in.

*George Bush*

---

There is nothing that gives a man consequence, and renders him fit for command, like a support that renders him independent of everybody but the state he serves.

*George Washington*

---

Let us remember that America was built not by government but by people, not by welfare, but by work, not by shirking responsibility, but by seeking responsibility.

*Richard M. Nixon*

You are not here merely to make a living. You are here in order to enable the world to live more amply, with greater vision, with a finer spirit of hope and achievement. You are here to enrich the world, and you impoverish yourself if you forget the errand.

*Woodrow Wilson*

We are a proudly idealistic nation, but let no one confuse our idealism with weakness.

*Jimmy Carter*

There is but one element of government, and that is The People. From this element springs all governments. For a nation to be free, it is only necessary that she wills it.

*John Adams*

Truth is the glue that holds our government together. Our long national nightmare is over. Our Constitution works.

*Gerald Ford*

We must do what America does best: offer more opportunity to all and demand more responsibility from all. It is to break the bad habit of expecting something for nothing from our Government  or from each other. Let us take more responsibility not for ourselves and our families but for our communities and our country.

***Bill Clinton***

I have not sought, I do not seek, I repudiate the support of any advocate of Communism or of any other alien "ism" which would by fair means or foul change our American democracy.

*Franklin D. Roosevelt*

---

You cannot have a decent government unless the majority exercise the self-restraint that men with great power ought to exercise.

*William Howard Taft*

---

May our country be always successful, but whether successful or otherwise, always right.

*John Quincy Adams*

---

I believe God had a divine purpose in placing this land between two great oceans to be found by those who had a special love of freedom and courage.

*Ronald Reagan*

---

I think that the real trick is how we can keep the basic values that have made our country great, and take advantage of the modern world with all the things that are different. That has always been the genius of America—to preserve what is right there in the Constitution, and to take it throughout history.

*Bill Clinton*

For more than half a century, during which kingdoms and empires have fallen, this Union has stood unshaken. The patriots who formed it have long since descended to the grave; yet still it remains, the proudest monument to their memory.

*Zachary Taylor*

---

The President is the representative of the whole nation and he's the only lobbyist that all one hundred and sixty million people in this country have.

*Harry S. Truman*

---

There is a power in public opinion in this country and I thank God for it; for it is the most honest and best of all powers which will not tolerate an incompetent or unworthy man to hold in his weak or wicked hands the lives and fortunes of his fellow citizens.

*Martin Van Buren*

---

The government is a partner, but the people, the people realize the possibility of this country and ensure its continuation from generation to generation.

*Bill Clinton*

---

Our Constitution rests upon the good sense of the people. This basis, weak as it may appear, has not yet been found to fail.

*John Quincy Adams*

Let us therefore animate and encourage each other, and show the whole world that a freeman, contending for liberty on his own ground, is superior to any slavish mercenary on earth.

*George Washington*

---

It is clear that our common mission, if we want to help people help themselves and strengthen this country, must be focused on a relentless determination to see that every American lives up to the fullest of his or her capacities. It is in our common interest.

*Bill Clinton*

---

Whatever America hopes to bring to pass in the world must first come to pass in the heart of America.

*Dwight D. Eisenhower*

---

We meet on democracy's front porch. A good place to talk as neighbors and as friends. This is a day when our nation is made whole, when our differences, for a moment, are suspended.

*George Bush*

---

We have found ourselves rich in goods, but ragged in spirit; reaching with magnificent precision for the moon but falling into raucous discord on earth. We are caught in war, wanting peace. We are torn by divisions, wanting unity.

*Richard M. Nixon*

# Policy and Philosophy

## Part Two

I do not believe we can repair the basic fabric of society until people who are willing to work have work. Work organizes life. It gives structure and discipline to life. It gives meaning and self-esteem to people who are parents. It gives a role model to children.

*Bill Clinton*

---

Four-fifths of all our troubles would disappear, if we would only sit down and keep still.

*Calvin Coolidge*

---

Fear is the foundation of most governments.

*John Adams*

---

The Chinese use two brush strokes to write the word "crisis." One stroke stands for danger; the other stands for opportunity. In a crisis, it's important to be aware of the danger but recognize the opportunity.

*Richard M. Nixon*

---

Truth is generally the best vindication against slander.

*Abraham Lincoln*

For labor, a short day is better than a short dollar.

*William McKinley*

—•—

We have to maintain inviolate the great doctrine of the inherent right of popular self-government; to render cheerful obedience to the laws of the land, to unite in enforcing their execution, and to frown indignantly on all combinations to resist them.

*Franklin Pierce*

—•—

Government exists to protect us from each other. Where it has gone beyond its limits is in deciding to protect us from ourselves.

*Ronald Reagan*

—•—

Every man wishes to pursue his occupation and enjoy the fruits of his labors with the least possible expense. When these things are accomplished, all the objects for which government ought to be established are answered.

*Thomas Jefferson*

—•—

In a government founded on the sovereignty of the people, the education of youth is an object of the first importance.

*James Monroe*

—•—

The essence of government is power; and power, lodged in human hands, will ever be liable to abuse.

*James Madison*

---

If a free society cannot help the many who are poor, it cannot save the few who are rich.

*John F. Kennedy*

---

Public virtue cannot exist without private virtue.

*John Adams*

---

I reject the cynical view that politics is a dirty business.

*Richard M. Nixon*

---

Don't listen to that tired, liberal, class-warfare rhetoric about soaking the rich. Hold on to your wallets.

*George Bush*

---

Few men have virtue enough to withstand the highest bidder.

*George Washington*

Responsibility is proportionate to opportunity.

*Woodrow Wilson*

———

We must open the doors of opportunity. But we must also equip our people to walk through those doors.

*Lyndon B. Johnson*

———

No personal consideration should stand in the way of performing a public duty.

*Ulysses S. Grant*

———

We have to take responsibility for the way the young people of this country look at the world, how they define right and wrong; how they define their dignity. The greatest human beings who have ever lived in the whole history of humanity were consistently abused by others, and they were great because they did not lash out. What is this madness that our children are being taught—that it is all right to take violent action against other people if they do something you don't like?

*Bill Clinton*

———

My primary motive in becoming President is to bring America back to God.

*Warren G. Harding*

———•———

One with the law is a majority.

*Calvin Coolidge*

———•———

What counts is not the size of the dog in the fight but the size of the fight in the dog.

*Dwight D. Eisenhower*

———•———

A President is neither prince nor pope, and I don't seek "a window on men's souls." In fact, I yearn for a greater tolerance, an easy-goingness about each other's attitudes and way of life.

*George Bush*

———•———

Fourscore and seven years ago our fathers brought forth on this continent a new nation, conceived in liberty and dedicated to the proposition that all men are created equal.

*Abraham Lincoln*

———•———

Public opinion is the most potent monarch this world knows.

*Benjamin Harrison*

———•———

Conscience is that magistrate of God in the human heart whose still small voice the loudest revelry cannot drown.

*William Henry Harrison*

---

The best epitaph I ever saw was on Butte Hill in Tombstone, Arizona. It said, "Here lies Jack Williams, he done his damnedest." What more can a man do?

*Harry S. Truman*

---

Children are our most valuable natural resource.

*Herbert Hoover*

---

Give the President control over the purse and the power to place the immense revenues of the country into any hands he may please, and I care not what you call him, he is every inch a king.

*John Tyler*

---

Our people want a President to be both tough and gentle, both statesman and politician, both dreamer and fighter.

*Jimmy Carter*

Let both sides seek to invoke the wonders of science instead of its terrors. Together let us explore the stars, conquer the deserts, eradicate disease, tap the ocean depths, and encourage the arts and commerce.

*John F. Kennedy*

———•———

Inflation is as violent as a mugger, as frightening as an armed robber, and as deadly as a hit man.

*Ronald Reagan*

———•———

I go for all sharing the privileges of the government with those who assist in bearing its burdens.

*Abraham Lincoln*

———•———

Facts are stubborn things; and whatever may be our wishes, our inclinations, or the dictates of our passions, they cannot alter the state of facts and evidence.

*John Adams*

———•———

He mocks the people who propose that the government shall protect the rich and that they, in turn, shall care for the poor.

*Grover Cleveland*

———•———

A typical vice of American politics is the avoidance of saying anything real on real issues.

*Theodore Roosevelt*

Civilization and profits go hand in hand.

*Calvin Coolidge*

The cornerstone of modern civilization must continue to be religion and morality.

*William Howard Taft*

Once we considered education a public expense; we know now that it is a public investment.

*Lyndon B. Johnson*

I am asking you to join with the American people in their call for change. My vision is one of fundamental change—to invest in people, to reward hard work and restore fairness, and to recognize our families and communities as the cornerstones of America's strength.

*Bill Clinton*

Vacillation and inconsistency are as incompatible with successful diplomacy as they are with the national dignity.

*Benjamin Harrison*

---

I believe that all the measures of the government are directed to the purpose of making the rich richer and the poor poorer.

*William Henry Harrison*

---

We must act on what we know. I take as my guide the hope of a saint: "In crucial things, unity—in important things, diversity—in all things, generosity."

*George Bush*

---

Let us have faith that right makes might, and in that faith let us, to the end, dare to do our duty as we understand it.

*Abraham Lincoln*

---

The spirit of democracy can survive only through universal education.

*Herbert Hoover*

The destruction of our state governments or the annihilation of their control over the local concerns of the people would lead directly to revolution and anarchy, and finally to despotism and military domination.

*Andrew Jackson*

In Congress, where there are more than one hundred talking lawyers, you make no calculation upon the termination of any debate, and frequently the more trifling the subject, the more animated and protracted the discussion.

*Franklin Pierce*

Let those of us who are well-fed, well-clothed, and well-housed never forget and never overlook those who live on the outskirts of hope.

*Lyndon B. Johnson*

Today we are nearer to the final triumph over poverty than ever before in the history of any land.

*Herbert Hoover*

Government exists to protect us from each other. Where it has gone beyond its limits is in deciding to protect us from ourselves.

*Ronald Reagan* p 35

I have a great veneration for religion but I cannot bear a hypocrite or a bigoted fanatic.

*James K. Polk*

———•———

Raised in unrivaled prosperity, we inherit an economy that is still the world's strongest, but is weakened by business failures, stagnant wages, increasing inequality, and deep divisions among our people.

**Bill Clinton**

———•———

America's present need is not heroics but healing; not nostrums but normalcy; not revolution but restoration; not surgery but serenity.

**Warren G. Harding**

———•———

I know no method to secure the repeal of bad or obnoxious laws so effective as their stringent execution.

*Ulysses S. Grant*

———•———

We have discovered that every child who learns, and every man who finds work, and every sick body that is made whole—like a candle added to an altar—brightens the hope of all the faithful.

**Lyndon B. Johnson**

Let us pray for the salvation of all those who live in totalitarian darkness and pray they will discover the joy of knowing God. But until they do, let us be aware that they are the focus of evil in the world.

*Ronald Reagan*

---

I think the government ought to stay out of the prayer business.

*Jimmy Carter*

---

Every gun that is made, every warship launched, every rocket fired signifies, in the final sense, a theft from those who hunger and are not fed, those who are cold and are not clothed.

*Dwight D. Eisenhower*

---

Talk to God about me every day by name and ask Him to give me strength for my great task.

*Warren G. Harding*

---

With malice toward none; with charity for all; with firmness in the right, as God gives us to see the right, let us strive on to finish the work we are in; to bind up the nation's wounds; to care for him who shall have borne the battle, and for his widow and his orphan, to do all which may achieve and cherish a just and lasting peace among ourselves, and with all nations.

*Abraham Lincoln*

A conservative is one who makes no changes and consults his grandmother when in doubt.

*Woodrow Wilson*

———•———

Nothing can now be believed which is seen in a newspaper. Truth itself becomes suspicious by being put into that polluted vehicle.

*Thomas Jefferson*

———•———

Education is about more than making money and mastering technology, even in the 21st century. It's about making connections and mastering the complexities of the world. It's about seeing the world as it is and advancing the cause of human dignity. Money without purpose leads to an empty life. Technology without compassion and wisdom and a devotion to truth can lead to nightmares.

*Bill Clinton*

———•———

If you would be a leader of men, you must lead your own generation, not the next.

*Woodrow Wilson*

———•———

Happiness lies not in the mere possession of money; it lies in the joy of achievement, in the thrill of creative effort.

*Franklin D. Roosevelt*

———•———

The American people will not buy political double-talk.

*Gerald Ford*

---

I believe that football, perhaps more than any other sport, tends to instill in men the feeling that victory comes through hard, slavish team play, self-confidence, and enthusiasm that amounts to dedication.

*Dwight D. Eisenhower*

---

Tranquility at home and peaceful relations abroad constitute the true permanent policy of our country.

*James K. Polk*

---

Once you've seen one redwood tree, you've seen them all.   HE DID

*Ronald Reagan*   NOT SAY
THIS!

---

Damn the Negroes. I am fighting these traitorous aristocrats, their masters.

*Andrew Johnson*

There is but one way for a President to deal with Congress, and that is continuously, incessantly, and without interruption. If it is really going to work, the relationship has got to be almost incestuous.

*Lyndon B. Johnson*

---

Fair play is a jewel.

*Abraham Lincoln*

---

I believe that our Great Maker is preparing the world, in His own good time, to become one nation, speaking one language.

*Grover Cleveland*

---

I want a leaner, not a meaner, government.

*Bill Clinton*

---

The mission of the United States is one of benevolent assimilation.

*William McKinley*

It is far better to dare mighty things, to win glorious triumphs, even though checkered by failure, than to take rank with those poor spirits who neither enjoy much nor suffer much, because they live in the gray twilight that knows neither victory nor defeat.

*Theodore Roosevelt*

---

Our form of government has no sense unless it is founded in a deeply felt religious faith.

*Dwight D. Eisenhower*

---

The moment the idea is admitted into society that property is not as sacred as the law of God...tyranny and anarchy commence.

*John Adams*

---

Nothing in the world can take the place of persistence. Talent will not; nothing is more common than unsuccessful men with talent. Genius will not; unrewarded genius is almost a proverb. Education alone will not; the world is full of educated derelicts. Persistence and determination alone are omnipotent.

*Calvin Coolidge*

Liberty is its own reward.

*Woodrow Wilson*

---

Peace, commerce, and honest friendship with all nations—entangling alliances with none.

*Thomas Jefferson*

---

Speak softly and carry a big stick.

*Theodore Roosevelt*

---

At the desk where I sit, I have learned one great truth. The answer to all our national problems—the answer to all the problems of the world—comes down to a single word. That word is education.

*Lyndon B. Johnson*

---

Ideas control the world.

*James A. Garfield*

I acknowledge Thy presence and Thy power, O blessed Spirit; in Thy Divine wisdom now erase my mortal limitations and from Thy pure substance of love bring into manifestation my world, according to Thy perfect law.

*Millard Fillmore*

———•———

All men having power ought to be mistrusted.

*James Madison*

———•———

Carry the battle to them. Don't let them bring it to you. Put them on the defensive and don't ever apologize for anything.

*Harry S. Truman*

———•———

The test of our progress is not whether we add more to the abundance of those who have much; it is whether we provide enough for those who have too little.

*Franklin D. Roosevelt*

———•———

A government big enough to give you everything you want is a government big enough to take from you everything you have.

*Gerald Ford*

———•———

Policy & Philosophy

Some see leadership as high drama and the sound of trumpets calling. And sometimes it is that. But I see history as a book with many pages—and each day we fill a page with acts of hopefulness and meaning.

*George Bush*

———

There are risks and costs to a program of action, but they are far less than the long-range risks and costs of comfortable inaction.

*John F. Kennedy*

———

Doubts are the stuff of great decisions, but so are dreams.

*Jimmy Carter*

———

I believe that the outlawing of prayer in our public schools is against the Constitution. This is a nation of God and it is still on our coin: In God We Trust.

*Ronald Reagan*

———

Prosperity is only an instrument to be used, not a deity to be worshiped.

*Calvin Coolidge*

It's easier to do a job right than to explain why you can't.

*Martin Van Buren*

———

We should not allow in city after city after city our police officers to go to work everyday knowing that they will walk the mean streets with people who are better armed than they are. Because this is the only country in the world where teenagers can have assault weapons designed only to kill other people, and use them with abandon on the streets of our cities. We can do better than that.

*Bill Clinton*

———

American business is not a monster. It is an expression of a God-given impulse to create; the savior of our happiness.

*Warren G. Harding*

———

I would keep as much money in the treasury as the safety of the Government required, and no more. I would bring the Government back to what it was intended to be—a plain, economical Government.

*James K. Polk*

———

The convention system has its faults, of course, but I do not know of a better method for choosing a Presidential nominee.

*Harry S. Truman*

———•———

If the tide of defamation and abuse shall turn, and my administration come to be praised, future vice-presidents who may succeed to the Presidency may feel some slight encouragement to pursue an independent course.

*John Tyler*

———•———

The entire graduated income tax system was created by Karl Marx.

*Ronald Reagan*

———•———

Get action. Do things; don't fritter away your time. Take a place wherever you are and be somebody.

*Theodore Roosevelt*

———•———

If we do not act to preserve what we now have…then nearly all of our children will be deprived of the enlarging and enriching contact with nature which is essential to the human spirit.

*Lyndon B. Johnson*

For mere vengeance I would do nothing. This nation is too great to look for mere revenge. But for the security of the future I would do everything.

*James A. Garfield*

———•———

Man in political life must be ambitious.

*Rutherford B. Hayes*

———•———

Don't join the book burners. Don't think you're going to conceal faults by concealing evidence that they never existed.

*Dwight D. Eisenhower*

———•———

When we are sick, we want an uncommon doctor; when we have a construction job to do, we want an uncommon engineer, and when we are at war, we want an uncommon general. It is only when we get into politics that we are satisfied with the common man.

*Herbert Hoover*

———•———

To contract new debts is not the way to pay old ones.

*George Washington*

———•———

My friends, we are not the sum of our possessions. They are not the measure of our lives. In our hearts we know what matters. We cannot hope only to leave our children a bigger car, a bigger bank account. We must hope to give them a sense of what it means to be a loyal friend, a loving parent, a citizen who leaves his home, his neighborhood, and town better than he found it.

*George Bush*

It is an unfortunate human failing that a full pocketbook often groans more loudly than an empty stomach.

*Franklin D. Roosevelt*

The men who succeed best in public life are those who take the risk of standing by their own convictions.

*James A. Garfield*

My fellow Americans, you gave me this job. And we're making progress on the things you hired me to do. But unless we reach deep inside to the values, the spirit, the soul, and the truth of human nature, none of the other things we seek to do will ever take us where we need to go.

*Bill Clinton*

Mere precedent is a dangerous source of authority.

*Andrew Jackson*

---

It is a national disgrace that our Presidents should be cast adrift and be compelled to keep a corner grocery for subsistence. We elect a man to the Presidency, expect him to be honest, to give up a lucrative profession, and after we have done with him we let him go into seclusion and perhaps poverty.

*Millard Fillmore*

---

If it is God's will that I must die by the hand of an assassin, I must be resigned. I must do my duty as I see it, and leave the rest with God.

*Abraham Lincoln*

---

The indiscriminate denunciation of the rich is mischievous. It perverts the mind, poisons the heart, furnishes an excuse for crime and no poor man was ever made richer or happier by it.

*Benjamin Harrison*

---

When you have read the Bible, you will know it is the word of God, because in it, you will have found the key to your own heart, your own happiness, and your own duty.

*Woodrow Wilson*

The best social program is a good job.

*Bill Clinton*

---

A people that values its privileges above its principles soon loses both.

*Dwight D. Eisenhower*

---

I should like to have it said of my first administration that in it the forces of selfishness and of lust for power met their match. I should like to have it said of my second administration that in it these forces met their master.

*Franklin D. Roosevelt*

---

The possession of great powers no doubt carries with it a contempt for mere external show.

*James A. Garfield*

---

Be brief; above all things, be brief.

*Calvin Coolidge*

There is a Democratic Party in America which is alive and well, a party committed to prosperity and opportunity for all America, a party more concerned with the future than the past, a party convinced we are living in changing times which require us to go beyond the established dogmas.

*Bill Clinton*

Public opinion: May it always perform one of its appropriate offices; by teaching the public functionaries of the state and federal government that neither shall assume the exercise of powers entrusted by the Constitution to the other.

*James K. Polk*

The effects of the late civil strife have been to free the slave and make him a citizen. Yet he is not possessed of the civil rights which citizenship should carry with it. This is wrong and should be corrected. To this correction I stand committed.

*Ulysses S. Grant*

The one continuing, unchanging, and unchangeable thing is character. A business built with conscience as its architect and character as its cornerstone is destined to stand foursquare and firm.

*Warren G. Harding*

We have earned the hatred of entrenched greed.

*Franklin D. Roosevelt*

---

There are many things in life that are not fair.

*Jimmy Carter*

---

The lessons of paternalism ought to be unlearned and a better lesson taught that, while the people should patriotically and cheerfully support their government, its functions do not include the support of the people.

*Grover Cleveland*

---

America is never wholly herself unless she is engaged in high moral principle. We as a people have such a purpose today. It is to make kinder the face of the nation and gentler the face of the world.

*George Bush*

---

From the first institution of government to the present time there has been a struggle going on between capital and labor for a fair distribution of profits resulting from their joint capacities.

*Martin Van Buren*

I have said to the people we mean to have less Government in business as well as more business in Government.

*Warren G. Harding*

———•———

I am one of those who do not believe that the national debt is a national blessing.

*Andrew Jackson*

———•———

The real American heroes today are the citizens who get up every morning and have the courage to work hard and play by the rules— the mother who stays up the extra half hour after a long day's work to read her child a story; the rescue worker who digs with his hands in the rubble as the building crumbles about him; the neighbor who lives side by side with people different from himself; the government worker who quietly and efficiently labors to see to it that the programs we depend on are honestly and properly carried out; most of all, the parent who works long years for modest pay and sacrifices so that his or her children can have the education and the chances you are going to have. I ask you never to forget that.

*Bill Clinton*

———•———

I had not the advantage of a classical education, and no man should, in my judgment, accept a degree he cannot read.

*Millard Fillmore*

(after refusing an honorary degree from Oxford University)

———•———

Policy & Philosophy

It's not what a man has, but what he is, that settles his class.

*Benjamin Harrison*

---

Abortion is advocated only by persons who have themselves been born.

*Ronald Reagan*

---

I pledge you, I pledge myself, to a new deal for the American people.

*Franklin D. Roosevelt*

---

Poverty has many roots, but the tap root is ignorance.

*Lyndon B. Johnson*

---

The people are the best guardians of their own rights and it is the duty of their Executive to abstain from interfering in the sacred exercise of the lawmaking functions of their government.

*William Henry Harrison*

---

He serves his party best who serves the country best.

*Rutherford B. Hayes*

In councils of government, we must guard against the acquisition of unwarranted influence, whether sought or unsought, by the military-industrial complex.

*Dwight D. Eisenhower*

All communities are apt to look to government for too much. The less government interferes with private pursuits, the better for the general prosperity.

*Martin Van Buren*

When people are thrown out of work unemployment results.

*Calvin Coolidge*

A revered President, long since dead, once told me that there was no solution to the relationship of the White House and the press and that there never would be a President who could satisfy them until he was twenty years dead.

*Herbert Hoover*

Rebellion to tyrants is obedience to God.

*Thomas Jefferson*

Let us be very clear on this matter; if we condemn people to inequality in our society we also condemn them to inequality in our economy.

*Lyndon B. Johnson*

---

We have heard the trumpets. We have changed the guard. And now each in our own way, and with God's help, must answer the call.

*Bill Clinton*

---

The ballot is stronger than the bullet.

*Abraham Lincoln*

---

I am running for President with a specific plan for economic change, a plan to jump-start our economy in the short term and a new long-term strategy to turn our country's economy around and restore the American Dream for all.

*Bill Clinton*

In order to have any success in life, you must resolve to carry into your work a fullness of knowledge, not merely a sufficiency, and be fit for more than what you are now doing. Let every one know that you have a reserve in yourself; that you have more power than you are now using. If you are not too large for the place you now occupy, you are too small for it.

*James A. Garfield*

I would suggest the taxation of all property equally whether it be church or corporation.

*Ulysses S. Grant*

Let every man pray that he may, in some true sense, be a soldier of fortune; that he may have the good fortune to spend his life in the service of his fellow men.

*Woodrow Wilson*

Each public officer who takes an oath to support the Constitution swears that he will support it as he understands, and not as it is understood by others.

*Andrew Jackson*

We cannot ever afford to rest at ease in the comfortable assumption that right ideas always prevail by some virtue of their own.

*Herbert Hoover*

---

The first object of my heart is my own country. In that is embarked my family, my fortune, and my existence.

*Thomas Jefferson*

---

Justice and good will will outlast passion.

*James A. Garfield*

---

My fellow Americans, a tree takes a long time to grow, and wounds take a long time to heal. But we must begin. Those who are lost now belong to God. Some day we will be with them. But until that happens, their legacy must be our lives.

*Bill Clinton*
*(said at memorial for Oklahoma bombing victims, April 23, 1995)*

---

In the discharge of the duties of this office, there is one rule of action more important than all others. It consists in never doing anything that someone else can do for you.

*Calvin Coolidge*

Just as ignorance breeds poverty, poverty all too often breeds ignorance in the next generation.

*Lyndon B. Johnson*

---

We should live our lives as though Christ was coming to visit us this very afternoon.

*Jimmy Carter*

---

The man who never looks into a newspaper is better informed than he who reads them; inasmuch as he who knows nothing is nearer the truth than he whose mind is filled with falsehoods.

*Thomas Jefferson*

---

You cannot be President of the United States if you don't have faith. Remember Lincoln, going to his knees in times of trial and the Civil War and all that stuff.

*George Bush*

---

Education makes a greater difference between man and man than nature has between man and brute.

*John Adams*

For of those to whom much is given, much is required.

*John F. Kennedy*

---

There is no grievance that is a fit object for redress by mob law.

*Abraham Lincoln*

---

On a candid examination of history, we shall find that turbulence, violence, and abuse of power by the majority have produced factions and commotions which have, more frequently than any other cause, produced despotism.

*James Madison*

---

We must believe in ourselves and our ability to shape our own destiny. Too many of us still expect too little of ourselves and demand too little of each other because we see the future as a question of fate, out of our hands. But the future need not be fate; it can be an achievement.

*Bill Clinton*

---

The foreign policy adopted by our government is to do justice to all, and to submit to wrong by none.

*Andrew Jackson*

Taste cannot be controlled by law.

*Thomas Jefferson*

Our differences are politics. Our agreements are principles.

*William McKinley*

Poverty not only strikes at the needs of the body. It attacks the spirit and it undermines human dignity.

*Lyndon B. Johnson*

There is one thing solid and fundamental in politics...the law of change. What is up today is down tomorrow.

*Richard M. Nixon*

Under our Constitution there is no connection between church and state, and as President, I recognize no distinction of creeds in my appointments to office.

*James K. Polk*

May God save the country; for it is evident that the people will not.

*Millard Fillmore*

The new rage is to say that the government is the cause of all of our problems, and if only we had no government, we'd have no problems. I can tell you, that contradicts evidence, history, and common sense.

*Bill Clinton*

---

The world is engaged in a race between education and chaos.

*Lyndon B. Johnson*

---

The chief business of America is business.

*Calvin Coolidge*

---

Perfectionism, no less than isolationism or imperialism or poor politics, may obstruct the paths to international peace.

*Franklin D. Roosevelt*

---

The things that will destroy America are prosperity-at-any-price, peace-at-any-price, safety-first instead of duty-first, the love of soft living, and the get-rich-quick theory of life.

*Theodore Roosevelt*

We Americans have no commission from God to police the world.

*Benjamin Harrison*

---

Unemployment insurance provides a prepaid vacation for a sector of our society which has made it a way of life.

*Ronald Reagan*

---

The will of the people is the best law.

*Ulysses S. Grant*

---

All across this country, there is a deep understanding rooted in our religious heritage and renewed in the spirit of this time that the bounty of nature is not ours to waste. It is a gift from God that we hold in trust for future generations.

*Bill Clinton*

---

Let justice be done, though heaven fall.

*John Quincy Adams*

---

The second office in the government is honorable and easy; the first is but a splendid misery.

*Thomas Jefferson*

A President cannot always be popular.

*Harry S. Truman*

---

Education is the result of contact. A great people is produced by contact with great minds.

*Calvin Coolidge*

---

Dollars and guns are no substitute for brains and willpower.

*Dwight D. Eisenhower*

---

Antisemitism is a noxious weed that should be cut out. It has no place in America.

*William Howard Taft*

---

I don't believe the President of the United States ought to debate with anybody.

*Lyndon B. Johnson*

---

Every person in this country who seeks to know and do the will of his or her Creator is entitled to respect for that effort.

*Bill Clinton*

A chicken in every pot.

*Herbert Hoover*

---

The power given by the Constitution to the Executive to interpose his veto is a high conservative power; but in my opinion, it should never be exercised except in cases of clear violation of the Constitution.

*Zachary Taylor*

---

We could cure the legislative diseases of senility and seniority if we limited the service of President, senator and congressman to twelve years.

*Harry S. Truman*

---

Republicans are men of narrow vision who are afraid of the future.

*Jimmy Carter*

---

It has always seemed to me that common sense is the real solvent for the nation's problems at all times. Common sense and hard work.

*Calvin Coolidge*

---

To me, party platforms are contracts with the people.

*Harry S. Truman*

Policy & Philosophy

A man to be a sound politician, and in any degree useful to his country, must be governed by higher and steadier considerations than those of personal sympathy and private regard.

*Martin Van Buren*

———

Constitutions are checks upon the hasty action of the majority.

*William Howard Taft*

———

When you play, play hard; when you work, don't play at all.

*Theodore Roosevelt*

———

There can be no greater error than to expect real favors from nation to nation.

*George Washington*

———

Words without action are the assassins of idealism.

*Herbert Hoover*

———

Read my lips; no new taxes.

*George Bush*

We must maintain the chance for contact with beauty. When that chance dies, a light dies in all of us.

*Lyndon B. Johnson*

—•—

There are times when the future seems thick as a fog; you sit and wait, hoping the mists will lift and reveal the right path. But this is a time when the future seems a door you can walk right through—into a room called Tomorrow.

*George Bush*

—•—

Our founders saw themselves in the light of posterity. We can do no less. Anyone who has ever watched a child's eyes wander into sleep, knows what posterity is. Posterity is the world to come: the world for whom we hold our ideals; from whom we have borrowed our planet, and to whom we bear sacred responsibility.

*Bill Clinton*

—•—

It is to be regretted that the rich and powerful too often bend the acts of government to their own selfish purposes.

*Andrew Jackson*

If political parties in a Republic are necessary to secure a degree of vigilance to keep the public functionaries within bounds of law and duty, at that point their usefulness ends.

*William Henry Harrison*

From the first institution of government to the present time there has been a struggle going on between capital and labor for a fair distribution of profits resulting from their joint capacities.

*Martin Van Buren*

We can not right matters by taking from one what he has honestly acquired to bestow upon another what he has not earned.

*Benjamin Harrison*

The business of the country is like the level of the ocean, from which all measurements are made of height and depth.

*James A. Garfield*

No proper legislation is to be expected as long as members of the Congress are engaged in procuring offices for their constituents.

*Rutherford B. Hayes*

I am now in the presence of pure Being, and immersed in the
Holy Spirit of life, love and wisdom.   *NOT TRUE*

*QUOTE FROM CHARLES* **Millard Fillmore**
*FILLMORE* *(Filmore's last words, said on his death bed)*

---

If American democracy is to remain the greatest hope of
humanity, it must continue abundantly in the faith of the Bible.

*Calvin Coolidge*

---

There are no necessary evils in government. Its evils exist only in
its abuses. If it would confine itself to equal protection, and, as
Heaven does its rain, shower its favors alike on the high and the
low, the rich and the poor, it would be an unqualified blessing.

*Andrew Jackson*

---

I want to see, above all, that this remains a country where someone can always get rich.

*Ronald Reagan*

---

Let them impeach and be damned!

*Andrew Johnson*

Profound and powerful forces are shaking and remaking our world. And the urgent question of our time is whether we can make change our friend and not our enemy.

*Bill Clinton*

---

If you want to make enemies, try to change something.

*Woodrow Wilson*

---

What in the name of conscience will it take to pass a truly effective gun control law? Now in this hour of tragedy, let us spell out our grief in constructive action.

*Lyndon B. Johnson*
(said on June 6, 1968 on the death of Robert Kennedy)

---

The reactionary is always willing to take a progressive attitude on any issue that is dead.

*Theodore Roosevelt*

---

Never trouble another for what you can do yourself.

*Thomas Jefferson*

A popular government, without popular information, or the means of acquiring it, is but a prologue to a farce or a tragedy.

*James Madison*

—•—

It is our responsibility to restore hope to our people. The voices of conventional wisdom will first whisper and then shout that it cannot be done. But we must summon the wisdom and courage to reject convention and embrace the new direction that we have needed for so long.

*Bill Clinton*

—•—

The whole of government consists in the art of being honest.

*Thomas Jefferson*

—•—

I do not mistrust the future; I do not fear what is ahead. For our problems are large, but our heart is larger. Our challenges are great, but our will is greater. And if our flaws are endless, God's love is truly boundless.

*George Bush*

—•—

The American Revolution was a beginning, not a consummation.

*Woodrow Wilson*

—•—

Policy & Philosophy

Whenever a man has cast a longing eye on an office, a rottenness begins in his conduct.

*Thomas Jefferson*

This Administration here and now declares unconditional war on poverty in America.

*Lyndon B. Johnson*

I cannot conceive of a wholesome social order or a sound economic system that does not have its roots in religious faith.

*Herbert Hoover*

Tyranny and despotism can be exercised by many, more rigorously, more vigorously, and more severely than by one.

*Andrew Johnson*

Let the farmer forevermore be honored in his calling; for they who labor in the earth are the chosen people of God.

*Thomas Jefferson*

# Humor and Humility
## Part Three

My country has, in its wisdom, contrived for me the most insignificant office that ever the invention of man contrived or his imagination conceived.

*John Adams*
(said of the vice-presidency)

---

The current tax code is like a daily mugging.

*Ronald Reagan*

---

If our country is to survive and prosper, we need the best efforts of all Americans—men and women—to bring it about. And besides, as a great philosopher once said—I think it was Henry Kissinger—nobody will ever win the Battle of the Sexes. There's just too much fraternizing with the enemy.

*Gerald Ford*

---

The President ought to be allowed to hang two men every year without giving any reason or explanation.

*Herbert Hoover*

I feel like the man who was tarred and feathered and ridden out of town on a rail. To the man who asked how he liked it he said: "If it wasn't for the honor of the thing, I'd rather walk."

*Abraham Lincoln*

---

I may be President of the United States, but my private life is nobody's damned business.

*Chester A. Arthur*

---

If you are as happy, my dear sir, on entering this house as I am in leaving it, you are the happiest man in the country.

*James Buchanan*
(to Abraham Lincoln)

---

To suddenly get my hair colored, and dance up and down in a miniskirt or do something, you know, show that I've got a lot of jazz out there and drop one-liners, I'm running for the President of the United States—I kind of think I'm a scintillating kind of fellow.

*George Bush*

---

I can get up at nine and be rested, or I can get up at six and be President.

*Jimmy Carter*

I like the job…The bad days are part of it. I didn't run to have a pleasant time. I ran to have the chance to change the country, and if the bad days come with it—that's part of life, and it's humbling and educational. It keeps you in your place.

*Bill Clinton*

---

I am not concerning myself about what history will think, but contenting myself with the approval of this fellow named Cleveland whom I have generally found to be a pretty good sort of fellow.

*Grover Cleveland*

---

If I ever tell a lie, if I ever mislead you, if I ever betray a trust or a confidence, I want you to come and take me out of the White House.

*Jimmy Carter*

---

The most pleasant thing I do is meeting people. It is the only fun I have.

*Warren G. Harding*

In the Middle Ages it was the fashion to wear hair shirts to remind one's self of trouble and sin. Many years ago I concluded that a few hair shirts were part of the mental wardrobe of every man. The President differs only from other men in that he has a more extensive wardrobe.

*Herbert Hoover*

While you're saving your face, you're losing your ass.

*Lyndon B. Johnson*

Within the first few months I discovered that being a President is very much like riding a tiger…You have to keep riding or be swallowed.

*Harry S. Truman*

All the extraordinary men I have ever known were extraordinary in their own estimation.

*Woodrow Wilson*

As to the Presidency, the two happiest days of my life were those of my entry upon the office and those of my surrender of it.

*Martin Van Buren*

It is not a custom with me to keep money to look at.

*George Washington*

---

Popularity, I have always thought, may aptly be compared to a coquette—the more you woo her, the more apt is she to elude your embrace.

*John Tyler*

---

When you come to the end of your rope, tie a knot and hang on.

*Franklin D. Roosevelt*

---

California is proud to be the home of the freeway.

*Ronald Reagan*

---

Families do not eat and breathe political slogans — they do not. Most families couldn't tell you for the life of them whether I'm up or down in the polls this week, and they couldn't care less. They just know whether they're up or down in their real life struggle this week. And that's what we ought to think about.

*Bill Clinton*

When the President does it, that means it is not illegal.

*Richard M. Nixon*

---

I have noticed that nothing I ever said ever did me any harm.

*Calvin Coolidge*

---

Being the President was the four most miserable years of my life.

*John Adams*

---

Government after all is a very simple thing.

*Warren G. Harding*

---

I'm a Ford, not a Lincoln.

*Gerald Ford*

---

The passion for office and the number of unworthy persons who seek to live on the public is increasing beyond former example, and I now predict that no President of the United States will ever again be re-elected. The reason is that the patronage of the government will destroy the popularity of any President, however well he may administer the government.

*James K. Polk*

I'm proud to be called a pig. It stands for pride, integrity, and guts.

*Ronald Reagan*

---

Jerry Ford is so dumb that he can't fart and chew gum at the same time.

*Lyndon B. Johnson*

---

What do Presidents do to pass the time? We spend our time taking pills and dedicating libraries.

*Herbert Hoover*

---

For years politicians have promised the moon—I'm the first one to be able to deliver it.

*Richard M. Nixon*
*(on the occasion of the first moon landing, July 20, 1969)*

---

There is an old saying that a man will never get into trouble if he keeps his mouth shut. I tried to keep mine shut about politics, but look at me—here I am.

*Dwight D. Eisenhower*

I was America's first instant Vice President—and now, America's first instant President. The Marine Corps Band is so confused, they don't know whether to play "Hail to the Chief" or "You've Come a Long Way, Baby."

*Gerald Ford*

—•—

Some people want champagne and caviar when they should have beer and hot dogs.

*Dwight D. Eisenhower*

—•—

My favorite animal is the mule. He has more horse sense than a horse. He knows when to stop eating and he knows when to stop working.

*Harry S. Truman*

—•—

Oh, what I perceive for this nation in the year 2000 is so exciting to me that I just hope the doctors hurry up and get busy and let me live that long.

*Lyndon B. Johnson*

—•—

A taxpayer is someone who works for the federal government but doesn't have to take a civil service examination.

*Ronald Reagan*

—•—

I have no expectation of making a hit every time I come to bat.

*Franklin D. Roosevelt*

---

My sympathy rises for the humble decimal point. His is a pathetic life, wandering around among regimented ciphers trying to find some of the old places he used to know.

*Herbert Hoover*

---

Had I been chosen President again, I am certain that I could not have lived another year.

*John Adams*

---

Never go out to meet trouble. If you will just sit still, nine cases out of ten, someone will intercept it before it reaches you.

*Calvin Coolidge*

---

If you think too much about being re-elected, it is very difficult to be worth re-electing.

*Woodrow Wilson*

I am a man of limited talents from a small town and I don't seem to grasp that I am President.

*Warren G. Harding*

—————

A political office seems like a hammock. It's hard to get into and even harder to get out of gracefully.

*Dwight D. Eisenhower*

—————

I mean to make myself a man, and if I succeed in that, I shall succeed in everything else.

*James A. Garfield*

—————

It is a pleasure to be here this morning to pay tribute to the American hardware industry. Yours is an industry that has taken American ingenuity and coupled it with some of the most effective merchandising techniques known to mortal man. Now that may seem like exaggeration, but a hardware store is the only business I know of where you can go to buy a ten-cent carriage bolt—and come out with a can of paint, a new improved screwdriver, 50 pounds of charcoal briquets, a bicycle tire kit, 10 minutes worth of free advice, 12 picture hooks, 6 fuses, and a lawn mower—and then have to go back because you forgot the ten-cent carriage bolt you went in to buy in the first place.

*Gerald Ford*

We meet in a historic hall tonight. In this very spot will be chosen an American leader for 1965, a person who symbolizes the American dream. I am sad that it becomes my duty to announce tonight that that person will not be me—it will be Miss America of 1965.

*Lyndon B. Johnson*

---

If you can't convince them; confuse them.

*Harry S. Truman*

---

I happen temporarily to occupy this big White House. I am a living witness that any one of your children may look to come here as my father's child has.

*Abraham Lincoln*

---

Once upon a time my political opponents honored me as possessing the fabulous intellectual and economic power by which I created a worldwide depression all by myself.

*Herbert Hoover*

---

I don't know much about Americanism, but it's a damned good word with which to carry an election.

*Warren G. Harding*

Fluency in English is something that I'm often not accused of.

*George Bush*

---

Now that all the members of the press are so delighted I lost, I would like to make a statement. As I leave you I want you to think about how much you'll be missing. You won't have Nixon to kick around anymore.

*Richard M. Nixon*

---

Humility must always be the portion of any man who receives acclaim earned in blood of his followers and sacrifices of his friends.

*Dwight D. Eisenhower*

---

You know all those Secret Service men you've seen around me? When I play golf, they get combat pay!

*Gerald Ford*

---

Assassination can be no more guarded against than death by lightning and it is best not to worry about either.

*James A. Garfield*

People who've had a hanging in the family don't like to talk about rope.

*Calvin Coolidge*

—•—

I know only two tunes; one of them is "Yankee Doodle," and the other isn't.

*Ulysses S. Grant*

—•—

Just forget that I am the President of the United States. I'm just Warren Harding playing poker with my friends and I'm going to beat the hell out of them.

*Warren G. Harding*

—•—

Ronald Reagan doesn't dye his hair—he's just prematurely orange.

*Gerald Ford*

—•—

I've got to run now and relax. The doctor told me to relax. The doctor told me to relax. The doctor told me. He was the one. He said, "Relax."

*George Bush*

There are only two occasions when Americans respect privacy, especially in Presidents. Those are prayer and fishing.

*Herbert Hoover*

———

Sure, it's a big job; but I don't know anyone who can do it better than I can.

*John F. Kennedy*

———

I smoked tobacco and read Milton at the same time, and from the same motive—to find out what was the charm in them which gave my father so much pleasure. After making myself four or five times sick with smoking, I mastered that accomplishment...but I did not master Milton.

*John Quincy Adams*

———

I can't make a damn thing out of this tax problem. I know somewhere there is an economist who knows the truth, but I don't know where to find him and haven't the sense to know him and trust him when I do find him. God! What a job.

*Warren G. Harding*

———

I'm not from Washington and I'm not a lawyer.

*Jimmy Carter*

Many folks are silly enough as to have formed a plan to make a President out of this clerk and clodhopper.

*William Henry Harrison*

---

The President is the last person in the world to know what the people really want and think.

*James A. Garfield*

---

If you don't say anything, you'll never be called upon to repeat it.

*Calvin Coolidge*

---

I am not liked as a President by the politicians in office, in the press or in Congress, but I am content to abide in the judgment and sober second thought of the people.

*Rutherford B. Hayes*

---

You may remember that in my early days I was a sort of bleeding-heart liberal. Then I became a man and put away childish ways.

*Ronald Reagan*

I have trouble with my enemies, but my goddam friends are the ones who keep me walking the floor at night.

*Warren G. Harding*

---

The beautiful Christmas tree you see out there came from Michigan. That tree and I have a lot in common. Neither one of us expected to be in the White House a few months ago, both of us were a little green, and we've both been trimmed a little lately.

*Gerald Ford*

---

I don't claim to know all of the answers.

*Jimmy Carter*

---

I would never read a book if it were at all possible for me to talk half an hour with the man who wrote it.

*Woodrow Wilson*

---

"Practical politics" means selfish ends promoted by base means.

*Rutherford B. Hayes*

Fishing is the chance to wash one's soul with pure air. It brings meekness and inspiration, reduces our egotism, soothes our troubles, and shames our wickedness. It is discipline in the equality of men; for all men are equal before fish.

*Herbert Hoover*

---

A long time ago down in Texas I learned that telling a man to go to hell and making him go there are two different propositions.

*Lyndon B. Johnson*

---

I should like to be known as a former President who minded his own business.

*Calvin Coolidge*

---

Only two things are necessary to keep a wife happy. One is to let her think she is having her way, and the other is to let her have it.

*Lyndon B. Johnson*

---

Private life would be a paradise compared to the best situation here; and if once more there, it would take a writ of habeas corpus to remove me into public life again.

*Andrew Jackson*

Do not bite at the bait of pleasure till you know there is no hook beneath it.

*Thomas Jefferson*

———

I claim not to have controlled events, but confess plainly that events have controlled me.

*Abraham Lincoln*

———

It is important that the United States remain a two-party system. I'm a fellow who likes small parties and the Republican Party can't be too small to suit me.

*Lyndon B. Johnson*

———

I'm not smart enough to lie.

*Ronald Reagan*

———

Public debt is paying for a dead horse. Private debt is buying a live one.

*Herbert Hoover*

I'm very grateful for this very unusual gift—a lamp made out of a phone. But I have to tell you, I'm a little worried about it. I'm in enough trouble now without saying to someone, "Excuse me, I have to answer the lamp." Oh…someone just told me the lamp works but the phone doesn't. That's all right. Maybe that's what we need these days—more light and less talk.

*Gerald Ford*

---

You will expect me to discuss the late election. Well, as nearly as I can learn, we did not have enough votes on our side.

**Herbert Hoover**

---

The French marshal Lyautey once asked his gardener to plant a tree. The gardener objected that the tree was slow growing and would not reach maturity for 100 years. The marshal replied, "In that case, there is no time to lose; plant it this afternoon."

**John F. Kennedy**

---

I think the American public wants a solemn ass as a president, and I think I'll go along with them.

**Calvin Coolidge**

---

If Kennedy runs, I'll whip his ass.

**Jimmy Carter**

The President last night had a dream. He was in a party of plain people, and as it became known who he was, they began to comment on his appearance. One of them said, "He is a common-looking man." The President replied, "Common-looking people are the best in the world; that is the reason the Lord makes so many of them."

*Abraham Lincoln*

---

You can tell a lot about a fellow's character by the way he eats jelly beans.

*Ronald Reagan*

---

I ask you to judge me by the enemies I have made.

*Franklin D. Roosevelt*

---

I am as strong as a bull moose, and you may use me to the limit.

*Theodore Roosevelt*

---

Mrs. Monroe hath added a daughter to our society who, though noisy, contributes greatly to its amusement.

*James Monroe*

When you have got an elephant by the hind leg, and he is trying to run away, it is best to let him run.

*Abraham Lincoln*

———————

My wife and I have the satisfaction that every dime we've got is honestly ours. I should say this, that Pat doesn't have a mink coat. But she does have a respectable Republican cloth coat, and I always tell her that she would look good in anything.

*Richard M. Nixon*

———————

I seldom think of politics more than eighteen hours a day.

*Lyndon B. Johnson*

———————

Governments have a tendency not to solve problems; only to rearrange them.

*Ronald Reagan*

———————

A bronco is something that kicks and bucks, twists and turns, and very seldom goes in one direction. We have one of those things here in Washington. It's called the Congress.

*Gerald Ford*

Love is the chain whereby to bind a child to his parents.

*Abraham Lincoln*

---

I used to say that politics was the second-oldest profession. I have come to know that it bears a gross similarity to the first.

*Ronald Reagan*

---

The only thing you have to worry about is bad luck and I never have bad luck.

*Harry S. Truman*

---

I never trust a man unless I've got his pecker in my pocket.

*Lyndon B. Johnson*

---

I never gave them hell. I just told the truth and they thought it was hell.

*Harry S. Truman*

---

Politics makes me sick.

*William Howard Taft*

I have a very wild golf swing. I'll tell you how wild my swing is. Back on my home course, they don't yell "Fore!" They yell "Ford!"

*Gerald Ford*

---

The idea that I should become President is too visionary to require a serious answer. It has never entered my head, nor is it likely to enter the head of any sane person.

*Zachary Taylor*

---

My choice early in life was either to be a piano player in a whorehouse or a politician. And to tell the truth, there's hardly any difference.

*Harry S. Truman*

---

I am only an average man, but, by George, I work harder at it than the average man.

*Theodore Roosevelt*

---

I desire to so conduct the affairs of this administration that if, at the end I have lost every friend on earth, I shall have one friend left, and that friend shall be down inside me.

*Abraham Lincoln*

The nine most terrifying words in the English language are "I'm from the government and I'm here to help."

*Ronald Reagan*

---

A President needs political understanding to run the government, but he may be elected without it.

*Harry S. Truman*

---

I don't have a handicap. I am all handicap.

*Lyndon B. Johnson*

---

Nobody has ever expected me to be President. In my poor, lean, lank face nobody has ever seen that any cabbages were sprouting out.

*Abraham Lincoln*

---

Here lies the body of my good horse, "The General." For twenty years he bore me around the circuit of my practice, and in all that time he never made a blunder. Would that his master could say the same.

*John Tyler*
*(On the grave of his horse)*

I hope I shall possess firmness and virtue enough to maintain what I consider the most enviable of all titles, the character of an honest man.

*George Washington*

---

I used to be a lawyer; now I am a reformed character.

*Woodrow Wilson*

---

Blessed are the young, for they shall inherit the national debt.

*Herbert Hoover*

---

Do you realize the responsibility I carry? I'm the only person standing between Richard Nixon and the White House.

*John F. Kennedy*

---

Ever since I was a youngster, I've had a special feeling for Kansas—because Kansas is where Dorothy lived before she went to visit the wonderful land of Oz—where all kinds of strange, whimsical, and unexpected things happened. But I'm beginning to think that if strange, whimsical, and unexpected things were what Dorothy was really interested in, she wouldn't have gone to Oz. She would have come to Washington.

*Gerald Ford*

Three things corrupt a man: power, money, and women. I never had but one woman in my life, and she's right at home. I never wanted power, and I never had any money, so I don't miss it.

*Harry S. Truman*

---

I will not make age an issue in this campaign. I am not going to exploit, for political purposes, my opponent's youth and inexperience.

*Ronald Reagan*

---

You don't have to tell me the latest jokes, Will, I appointed them.

*Warren G. Harding*
*(To Will Rogers)*

---

When you are asked if you can do a job, tell 'em, "Certainly I can!" Then get busy and find out how to do it.

*Theodore Roosevelt*

---

Bureaucracy rushes headlong into visions of the millennium and sends the bill to the Treasury.

*Herbert Hoover*

I may not know much, but I do know chicken shit from chicken salad.

*Lyndon B. Johnson*

When a President begins to worry about his image, he becomes like an athlete who's so concerned about what is said about him that he doesn't play the game well. I don't worry about my image or what the polls say, and I never have.

*Richard M. Nixon*

I think I might as well give up being a candidate. There are so many people in the country who don't like me.

*William Howard Taft*

A politician is a man who understands government. A statesman is a politician who's been dead for fifteen years.

*Harry S. Truman*

# Freedom, War and Peace
## Part Four

Individual liberty is individual power, and as a community is a mass compounded of individual powers. The nation which enjoys the most freedom must necessarily be in proportion to its numbers the most powerful nation.

*John Quincy Adams*

---

In war we offer our very lives as a matter of routine. We must be no less daring in the pursuit of peace.

*Jimmy Carter*

---

We have met the enemy and we are theirs!

*James Buchanan*

---

The challenge for this generation is to remember the deeds of those who served before and now build on their work in a new and very different world. The world wars are over. The Cold War has been won. Now it is our job to win the peace.

*Bill Clinton*

---

There is no substitute for a militant freedom.

*Calvin Coolidge*

All my life I have fought against prejudice and intolerance.

*Harry S. Truman*

———•———

Men may die, but the fabric of our free institutions remains unshaken. No higher or more assuring proof could exist of the strength and permanence of popular government than the fact that though the chosen of the people be struck down, his constitutional successor is peacefully installed without shock or strain except the sorrow which mourns the bereavement.

*Chester A. Arthur*

———•———

A new breeze is blowing, and a world refreshed by freedom seems reborn; for in man's heart, if not in fact, the day of the dictator is over. The totalitarian era is passing, its old ideas blown away like leaves from an ancient, lifeless tree. A new breeze is blowing, and a nation refreshed by freedom stands ready to push on. There is new ground to be broken, and a new action to be taken.

*George Bush*

———•———

Our security is not a matter of weapons alone. The arm that wields them must be strong, the eye that guides them clear, and the will that directs them indomitable.

*Franklin D. Roosevelt*

———•———

I have never advocated war except as a means of peace.

*Ulysses S. Grant*

—————

It is a paradox that every dictator has climbed to power on the ladder of free speech, and immediately on attaining that power each dictator has suppressed all free speech except his own.

*Herbert Hoover*

—————

There is enough in the world for everyone to have plenty to live on happily and to be at peace with his neighbors.

*Harry S. Truman*

—————

Guns, bombs, rockets and warships are all symbols of human failure. They are necessary symbols. They protect what we cherish. But they are witness to human folly.

*Lyndon B. Johnson*

—————

We cherish our friendship with all nations that would be free. And when, in time of want or peril, they ask our help, they may honorably receive it; for we no more seek to buy their sovereignty than we would sell our own.

*Dwight D. Eisenhower*

A standing army is one of the greatest mischiefs that can possibly happen.

*James Madison*

As long as our government is administered for the good of the people, and is regulated by their will; as long as it secures to us the rights of person and of property, liberty of conscience, and of the press, it will be worth defending.

*Andrew Jackson*

I would a thousand times rather march under a bloody shirt, stained with the lifeblood of a Union soldier, than to march under the black flag of treason or the white flag of compromise.

*Benjamin Harrison*

Only a peace between equals can last.

*Woodrow Wilson*

If there is not the war, you don't get the great general; if there is not a great occasion, you don't get the great statesman; if Lincoln had lived in a time of peace, no one would have known his name.

*Theodore Roosevelt*

The truth is found when men are free to pursue it.

*Franklin D. Roosevelt*

Freedom and the dignity of the individual have been more available and assured here than in any other place on Earth. The price for this freedom at times has been high. But we have never been unwilling to pay that price. As for the enemies of freedom, those who are potential adversaries, they will be reminded that peace is the highest aspiration of the American people. We will negotiate for it, sacrifice for it; we will not surrender for it now or ever.

*Ronald Reagan*

He who would be no slave must consent to have no slave. Those who deny freedom to others deserve it not for themselves, and under a just God, cannot long retain it.

*Abraham Lincoln*

Liberty unregulated by law degenerates into anarchy, which soon becomes the most horrid of all despotisms.

*Millard Fillmore*

Equality—the informing soul of freedom!

*James A. Garfield*

———•———

Liberty, according to my metaphysics, is a self-determining power in an intellectual agent. It implies thought, choice, and power.

*John Adams*

———•———

The only way to win World War III is to prevent it.

*Dwight D. Eisenhower*

———•———

Discipline is the soul of an army. It makes small numbers formidable; procures success to the weak, and esteem to all.

*George Washington*

———•———

The individual who refuses to defend his rights when called by his government deserves to be a slave, and must be punished as an enemy of his country.

*Andrew Jackson*

———•———

Many, if not most, of our Indian wars have had their origin in broken promises and acts of injustice on our part.

*Rutherford B. Hayes*

---

I hate war as only a soldier who has lived it can, as only one who has seen its brutality, its futility and its stupidity.

*Dwight D. Eisenhower*

---

Peace, after all, is the bedrock of all our hopes. Without peace, all of our work and progress comes to naught.

*Lyndon B. Johnson*

---

America, in the assembly of nations, has uniformly spoken among them the language of equal liberty, equal justice, and equal rights.

*John Quincy Adams*

---

The art of war is simple enough. Find out where your enemy is. Get at him as soon as you can. Strike him as hard as you can, and keep moving.

*Ulysses S. Grant*

Secrecy and a free, democratic government don't mix.
*Harry S. Truman*

---

War is a blessing compared with national degradation.
*Andrew Jackson*

---

There is nothing I love as much as a good fight.
*Franklin D. Roosevelt*

---

If we heed the teachings of history, we shall not forget that in the life of every nation emergencies may arise when a resort to arms can alone save it from dishonor.
*Chester A. Arthur*

---

True individual freedom cannot exist without economic security and independence. People who are hungry and out of a job are stuff of which dictatorships are made.
*Franklin D. Roosevelt*

The tree of Liberty must be refreshed from time to time with the blood of patriots and tyrants. It is their natural manure.

*Thomas Jefferson*

---

There is no security for the personal or political rights of any man in a community where that man is deprived of his personal or political rights.

*Benjamin Harrison*

---

See to the government. See that the government does not acquire too much power. Keep a check upon your rulers. Do this, and liberty is safe.

*William Henry Harrison*

---

Fighting battles is like courting girls; those who make the most pretensions and are boldest usually win.

*Rutherford B. Hayes*

---

A man with power and no conscience, could, with an eloquent tongue, put this whole country into flames.

*Woodrow Wilson*

Today our mission is to expand freedom's reach forward; to test the full potential of each of our own citizens; to strengthen our families, our faith, and our communities; to fight indifference and intolerance; to keep our nation strong; and to light the lives of those still dwelling in the darkness of undemocratic rule. Our parents did that and more; we must do nothing less.

*Bill Clinton*

Freedom of men's minds and souls is more precious to the future of humanity than even the jam on their bread.

*Herbert Hoover*

Morale is the greatest single factor in a successful war.

*Dwight D. Eisenhower*

Our policy is always to promote peace. We shall enter into any war with a full consciousness of the awful consequences that it always entails, whether successful or not, and we, of course, shall make every effort consistent with national honor and the highest national interest to avoid a resort to arms.

*William Howard Taft*

Peace, above all things, is to be desired, but blood must sometimes be spilled to obtain it on equable and lasting terms.

*Andrew Jackson*

---

In the field of world policy I would dedicate this nation to the policy of the good neighbor.

*Franklin D. Roosevelt*

---

The chief danger which threatens the influence and honor of the press is the tendency of its liberty to degenerate into license.

*James A. Garfield*

---

Concentrated power has always been the enemy of liberty.

*Ronald Reagan*

---

The history of liberty is the history of resistance.

*Woodrow Wilson*

---

Our liberty depends upon the freedom of the press, and that cannot be limited without being lost.

*Thomas Jefferson*

To place any dependence upon militia is, assuredly, resting upon a broken staff.

*George Washington*

—————

I like to believe that people, in the long run, are going to do more to promote peace than our governments. Indeed, I think that people want peace so much that one of these days governments had better get out of their way and let them have it.

*Dwight D. Eisenhower*

—————

We must build a new world, a far better world; one in which the eternal dignity of man is respected.

*Harry S. Truman*

—————

War is a contagion.

*Franklin D. Roosevelt*

—————

When people are oppressed by their government, it is a natural right they enjoy to relieve themselves of that oppression, and if they are strong enough, to overthrow it and substitute a more acceptable government.

*Ulysses S. Grant*

—— • ——

Error of opinion may be tolerated where reason is left free to combat it.

*Thomas Jefferson*

When people talk of freedom of writing, speaking, or thinking I cannot choose but laugh. No such thing ever existed. No such thing now exists; but I hope it will exist.

*John Quincy Adams*

On this tenth day of June 1940 the hand that held the dagger has struck it into the back of its neighbor.

*Franklin D. Roosevelt*

Because we are free we can never be indifferent to the fate of freedom elsewhere.

*Jimmy Carter*

Our society will not be great until every young mind is set free to scan the farthest reaches of thought and imagination.

*Lyndon B. Johnson*

We know what works: freedom works. We know what's right: freedom is right. We know how to secure a more just and prosperous life for men on earth: through free markets, free speech, free elections, and the exercise of free will unhampered by the state.

*George Bush*

———•———

There must be, not a balance of power, but a community of power; not organized rivalries, but an organized common peace.

*Woodrow Wilson*

———•———

Equal and exact justice to all men, of whatever state or persuasion, religious or political; peace, commerce, and honest friendship with all nations.

*Thomas Jefferson*

———•———

Let us never negotiate out of fear, but let us never fear to negotiate.

*John F. Kennedy*

———•———

The release of atomic energy constitutes a new force too revolutionary to consider in the framework of old ideas.

*Harry S. Truman*

———•———

A well-instructed people can be a free people.

*James Madison*

---

If slavery must end by war, let war come.

*John Quincy Adams*

---

No man is good enough to govern another man without that other's consent.

*Abraham Lincoln*

---

Just as freedom has a price, it also has a purpose, and its name is progress.

*Bill Clinton*

---

We must be ready to dare all for our country. For history does not long entrust the care of freedom to the weak or the timid.

*Dwight D. Eisenhower*

---

There was never a time when some way could not be found to prevent the drawing of the sword.

*Ulysses S. Grant*

No nation ever had an army large enough to guarantee it against attack in time of peace or insure it victory in time of war.

*Calvin Coolidge*

---

Our greatest happiness does not depend on the condition of life in which chance has placed us, but is always the result of a good conscience, good health, occupation, and freedom in all just pursuits.

*Thomas Jefferson*

---

War should never be entered upon until every agency of peace has failed.

*William McKinley*

---

I consider myself a deeply committed pacifist.

*Richard M. Nixon*

---

When you appeal to force, there's one thing you must never do...lose.

*Dwight D. Eisenhower*

A government never loses anything by mildness and forbearance to its own citizens, more especially when the consequences of an opposite course may be the shedding of blood.

*John Tyler*

---

May the turbulence of our age yield to a true time of peace, when men and nations shall share a life that honors the dignity of each and the brotherhood of all.

*Dwight D. Eisenhower*

---

Sixteen hours ago an American airplane dropped one bomb on Hiroshima. The force from which the sun draws its powers has been used against those who brought war to the Far East.

*Harry S. Truman*

---

All free men, wherever they may live, are citizens of Berlin. And therefore as a free man, I take pride in the words "Ich bin ein Berliner."

*John F. Kennedy*

---

Preparation for war is a constant stimulus to suspicion and ill will.

*James Monroe*

Don't hit at all if it's honorably possible to avoid hitting; but never hit soft!

*Theodore Roosevelt*

———

We have nothing in our history to invite aggression; we have everything to beckon us to the cultivation of relations of peace and amity with all nations.

*Franklin Pierce*

———

The blessings of liberty which our constitution secures may be enjoyed alike by minorities and majorities.

*James K. Polk*

———

Liberty is the means in the pursuit of happiness.

*William Howard Taft*

———

There is always inequity in life. Some men are killed in a war and some men are wounded and some men never leave the country... Life is unfair.

*John F. Kennedy*

———

In the final choice, a soldier's pack is not so heavy a burden as a prisoner's chains.

*Dwight D. Eisenhower*

There is no law saying the Negro has to live in Harlem or Watts.

*Ronald Reagan*

Unless justice is done to others it will not be done to us.

*Woodrow Wilson*

Justice is the end of government. It ever has been and ever will be pursued until it is obtained, or until liberty be lost in the pursuit.

*James Madison*

No man is above the law and no man is below it; nor do we ask any man's permission when we ask him to obey it.

*Theodore Roosevelt*

The passion for freedom is on the rise. Tapping this new spirit, there can be no nobler nor more ambitious task for America to undertake, on this day of a new beginning, than to help shape a just and peaceful world that is truly humane.

*Jimmy Carter*

---

The wave of the future is not the conquest of the world by a single dogmatic creed but the liberation of the diverse entities of free nations and free men.

*John F. Kennedy*

---

The American continents are henceforth not to be considered as subjects for future colonization by any European powers.

*James Monroe*

---

Freedom cannot be censored into existence. A democracy smugly disdainful of new ideas would be a sick democracy. A democracy chronically fearful of new ideas would be a dying democracy.

*Dwight D. Eisenhower*

No government ought to be without censors; and where the press is free, no one ever will.

*Thomas Jefferson*

———◆———

Let us all labor for free speech, free press, pure morals, unfettered religious sentiments, equal rights, and privileges for all men, irrespective of nationality, color, or religion.

*Ulysses S. Grant*

———◆———

The responsibility of the great states is to serve and not to dominate the world.

*Harry S. Truman*

———◆———

We know that when censorship goes beyond the observance of common decency…it quickly becomes, for us, a deadly danger.

*Dwight D. Eisenhower*

———◆———

A free man cannot be long an ignorant man.

*William McKinley*

———•———

We owe it therefore to candor, and to the amicable relations existing between the United States and those powers to declare that we should consider any attempt on their part to extend their system to any portion of this hemisphere as dangerous to our peace and safety.

*James Monroe*

---

I have seen war...I hate war.

*Franklin D. Roosevelt*

---

Patronage is the sword and cannon by which war may be made on the liberty of the human race.

*John Tyler*

---

I believe there are more instances of the abridgment of the freedom of the people by gradual and silent encroachments of those in power than by violent and sudden usurpations.

*James Madison*

---

I hold it that a little rebellion now and then is a good thing, and as necessary in the political world as storms in the physical.

*Thomas Jefferson*

To be prepared for war is one of the most effectual means of preserving peace.

*George Washington*

---

What a perversion of the normal order of things…to make power the primary object of the social system, and liberty but its satellite.

*James Madison*

# Odds and Ends

## Part Five

As the happiness of the people is the sole end of government, so the consent of the people is the only foundation of it.

*John Adams*

---

We have to deal with the appalling fact that, though thousands of lives have been sacrificed and hundreds of millions of dollars expended in the attempt to solve the Indian problem, it has, until within the past few years, seemed scarcely nearer a solution than it was half a century ago.

*Chester A. Arthur*

---

I shall carry to my grave the consciousness that I, at least, meant well for my country.

*James Buchanan*

---

To write off the United Nations' achievements in keeping the peace because of its inability to be effective in Czechoslovakia or Vietnam, would be like writing off medical science because it has not yet found a cure for cancer.

*George Bush*

Nothing is easier than spending public money. It does not appear to belong to anybody. The temptation is overwhelming to bestow it on somebody.

*Calvin Coolidge*

---

No person will have occasion to complain of want of time who never loses any.

*Thomas Jefferson*

---

When I finish my term, I want black people to say that I did more for them than any other President in their lifetime.

*Jimmy Carter*

---

A Republic without parties is a complete anomaly. The history of all popular governments show how absurd is the idea of their attempting to exist without parties.

*Franklin Pierce*

---

It's time you had a President who cares, takes responsibility, and knows what he wants to do with America for a change. You deserve more than slogans and 30-second TV commercials. You deserve more than political rhetoric and outdated proposals.

*Bill Clinton*

We shall sooner have the bird by hatching the egg than by smashing it.

*Abraham Lincoln*

---

It was involuntary. They sank my boat.

*John F. Kennedy*

---

In acquiring knowledge there is one thing equally important, and that is character. Nothing in the world is worth so much, will last so long, and serve its possessor so well as good character.

*William McKinley*

---

What is the use of being elected unless you stand for something.

*Grover Cleveland*

---

It is much easier to avoid disagreement than to remove discontents.

*George Washington*

---

I put confidence in the American people, in their ability to sort through what is fair and what is unfair, what is ugly and what is unugly.

*George Bush*

If you can't stand the heat get out of the kitchen.
*Harry S. Truman*

---

Never attempt to murder a man who is committing suicide.
*Woodrow Wilson*

---

There is no indispensable man.
*Franklin D. Roosevelt*

---

Politics is such a torment that I advise everyone I love not to mix
with it.

*Thomas Jefferson*

---

In life, as in a football game, the principle to follow is: Hit the
line hard.

*Theodore Roosevelt*

---

The best way to give advice to your children is to find out what
they want and then advise them to do it.

*Harry S. Truman*

If you want to send a man to the moon, send a Peace Corps member. It's an underdeveloped country.

*Dwight D. Eisenhower*

———•———

Sensible and responsible women do not want to vote. The relative positions to be assumed by man and woman in working out of our civilization were assigned long ago by a higher intelligence than ours.

*Grover Cleveland*

———•———

I cannot think of a single international or diplomatic achievement that's been realized by Ronald Reagan.

*Jimmy Carter*

———•———

Satisfaction does not come from indulgence; it comes from achievement.

*Calvin Coolidge*

———•———

As our 200th anniversary approaches, we owe it to ourselves and to posterity to rebuild our political and economic strength. Let us make America again, and for centuries more to come, what it has so long been—a stronghold and a beacon light of liberty for the whole world.

*Gerald Ford*

Be sincere; be brief; be seated.

*Franklin D. Roosevelt*

---

History is but the unrolled scroll of prophecy.

*James A. Garfield*

---

I propose to fight it out on this line if it takes all summer.

*Ulysses S. Grant*

---

Two Presidents or three, with equal powers, would as surely bring disaster as three generals of equal rank in a single army.

*Benjamin Harrison*

---

The basic principles laid down in the Ten Commandments are as applicable today as when they were declared, but they require  a host of subsidiary clauses. The ten ways to evil in the time of Moses have increased to ten thousand now.

*Herbert Hoover*

---

Few men are satisfied with less power than they are able to procure.

*William Henry Harrison*

Opposition and calumny are often the brightest tribute that vice and folly can pay to virtue and wisdom.

*Rutherford B. Hayes*

---

The only thing we have to fear is fear itself.

*Franklin D. Roosevelt*

---

Uncompromising thought is the luxury of the closeted recluse.

*Woodrow Wilson*

---

A leader has to lead, or otherwise he has no business in politics.

*Harry S. Truman*

---

Let me ask you to pray for the President that he will have the wisdom to change when he is wrong, the courage to stay the course when he is right, and somehow, somehow, the grace of God not to use the power of words at a time in human history when words are more omnipresent and more powerful than ever before, to divide and destroy, but instead to pierce to the truth, to the heart, to the best that is in us all.

*Bill Clinton*

It is time for a new generation of leadership to cope with new problems and new opportunities for there is a new world to be won.

*John F. Kennedy*

Never before have we had so little time in which to do so much.

*Franklin D. Roosevelt*

What we need is appointive positions in men of knowledge and experience who have sufficient character to resist temptations.

*Calvin Coolidge*

Delay is preferable to error.

*Thomas Jefferson*

One man with courage makes a majority.

*Andrew Jackson*

A decent and manly examination of the acts of government should not only be tolerated, but encouraged.

*William Henry Harrison*

It is wonderful how much may be done if we are always doing.

*Thomas Jefferson*

---

For the first time in this century—for the first time in perhaps all history—man does not have to invent a system by which to live. We don't have to talk late into the night about which form of government is better. We don't have to wrest justice from the kings. We only have to summon it from within ourselves.

*George Bush*

---

In my opinion, we are in danger of developing a cult of the common man, which means a cult of mediocrity.

*Herbert Hoover*

---

The Presidency does not yield to definition. Like the glory of a morning sunrise, it can only be experienced; it cannot be told.

*Calvin Coolidge*

---

Keep your eyes on the stars and your feet on the ground.

*Theodore Roosevelt*

I am not the most articulate emotionalist.

*George Bush*

———•———

The future is not an inheritance, it is an opportunity and an obligation.

*Bill Clinton*

———•———

Crises can indeed be agony. But it is the exquisite agony which a man might not want to experience again—yet would not for the world have missed.

*Richard M. Nixon*

———•———

This generation of Americans has a rendezvous with destiny.

*Franklin D. Roosevelt*

———•———

Progress is changing from a full dinner pail to a full garage.

*Herbert Hoover*

———•———

To deal with individual human needs at the everyday level can be noble sometimes.

*Jimmy Carter*

———•———

Odds & Ends

A President's hardest task is not to do what is right, but to know what is right.

*Lyndon B. Johnson*

---

Nothing is troublesome that we do willingly.

*Thomas Jefferson*

---

Every night when I go to bed I ask myself; what did we do today that we can point to for generations to come, to say that we laid the foundation for a better and more peaceful and more prosperous world?

*Lyndon B. Johnson*

---

A century has passed since the day of promise. The time of justice now has come.

*Lyndon B. Johnson*

---

Towering genius disdains a beaten path. It seeks regions hitherto unexplored.

*Abraham Lincoln*

A President either is constantly on top of events, or if he hesitates, events will soon be on top of him. I never felt that I could let up for a single moment.

*Harry S. Truman*

---

Do what you can where you are with what you've got.

*Theodore Roosevelt*

---

No President, no government, can teach us to remember what is best in what we are. But if the man you have chosen to lead this government can help make a difference; if he can celebrate the quieter, deeper successes that are made not of gold and silk, but of better hearts and finer souls; if he can do these things, then he must.

*George Bush*

---

There is no greater honor that can come to a man than to have a school named for him.

*Herbert Hoover*

---

All great changes are irksome to the human mind, especially those which are attended with great dangers.

*John Adams*

When a great ship cuts through the sea, the waters are always stirred and troubled. And our ship is moving through troubled new waters, toward new and better shores.

*Lyndon B. Johnson*

---

The great human advances have not been brought about by mediocre men and women. They were brought about by distinctly uncommon people with vital sparks of leadership.

*Herbert Hoover*

---

✳ Look to the economy of the mother and if you find it in her, you will find it in the daughter.

*Andrew Jackson*

---

To renew America, we must be bold.

*Bill Clinton*

---

Leadership and learning are indispensable to each other.

*John F. Kennedy*

Labor to keep alive in your breast that little spark of celestial fire called conscience.

*George Washington*

———

Those who hate you don't win unless you hate them...and that's when you destroy yourself.

*Richard M. Nixon*

———

The buck stops here.

*Harry S. Truman*

———

This beautiful capital, like every capital since the dawn of civilization, is often a place of intrigue and calculation. Powerful people maneuver for position and worry endlessly about who is in and who is out, who is up and who is down, forgetting those people whose toil and sweat sends us here and pays our way.

*Bill Clinton*

———

When angry, count ten before you speak; if very angry, a hundred.

*Thomas Jefferson*

The ideals of yesterday are the truths of today.

*William McKinley*

---

Nine-tenths of wisdom consists in being wise in time.

*Theodore Roosevelt*

---

I come before you and assume the Presidency at a moment rich with promise. We live in a peaceful, prosperous time, but we can make it better.

*George Bush*

---

The art of life is the avoiding of pain.

*Thomas Jefferson*

---

I've been kissing asses all my life and I don't have to kiss them anymore.

*Lyndon B. Johnson*

---

Most of the problems a President has to face have their roots in the past.

*Harry S. Truman*

Associate yourself with men of good quality if you esteem your own reputation for it is better to be alone than in bad company.
*George Washington*

Don't try to take on a new personality; it doesn't work.
*Richard M. Nixon*

Eternal truths will be neither true nor eternal unless they have fresh meaning for every new social situation.
*Franklin D. Roosevelt*

We never repent for having eaten too little.
*Thomas Jefferson*

It is common sense to take a method and try it. If it fails, admit it frankly and try another. But above all, try something.
*Franklin D. Roosevelt*

I find the remark, "'Tis distance lends enchantment to the view" is no less true of the political than of the natural world.
*Franklin Pierce*

Nothing in life is so exhilarating as to be shot at without result.

*Ronald Reagan*

---

The world moves, and ideas that were good once are not always good.

*Dwight D. Eisenhower*

---

I'll never get credit for anything I do in foreign policy because I didn't go to Harvard.

*Lyndon B. Johnson*

---

I have the honor of being the first Eagle Scout President of the United States.

*Gerald Ford*

---

Never buy what you do not want because it is cheap; it will be dear to you.

*Thomas Jefferson*

---

All the wastes in a year from a nuclear power plant could be stored under my desk.

*Ronald Reagan*

The most dangerous animal in the United States is the man with an emotion and a desire to pass a new law.

*Herbert Hoover*

A brilliant diversity spreads like the stars, like a thousand points of light in a broad and peaceful sky.

*George Bush*

I tell you, my friends, as certainly as it was true 200 years ago today, yesterday is yesterday. If we try to recapture it, we will only lose tomorrow.

*Bill Clinton*

The Soviet Union as everybody who has the courage to face the fact knows is run by a dictatorship as absolute as any other dictatorship in the world.

*Franklin D. Roosevelt*

Let us have faith that right makes might, and in that faith let us, to the end, dare to do our duty as we understand it.

*Abraham Lincoln*

I want to make an important policy statement. I am unabashedly in favor of women.

*Lyndon B. Johnson*

---

The one unchangeable certainty, is that nothing is unchangeable or certain.

*John F. Kennedy*

---

I am about to die. I expect the summons very soon. I have tried to discharge all my duties faithfully. I regret nothing, but am sorry that I am about to leave my friends.

*Zachary Taylor*

---

Once a decision was made, I did not worry about it afterward.

*Harry S. Truman*

---

The second sober thought of the people is seldom wrong and always efficient.

*Martin Van Buren*

Never put off till tomorrow what you can do today.
*Thomas Jefferson*

---

Every time an artist dies part of the vision of mankind passes with him.

*Franklin D. Roosevelt*

---

True friendship is a plant of slow growth, and must undergo and withstand the shocks of adversity before it is entitled to the appellation.

*George Washington*

---

Just as our security cannot rest on a hollow army, neither can it rest upon a hollow economy.

*Bill Clinton*

---

When we got into office, the thing that surprised me most was to find that things were just as bad as we'd been saying they were.

*John F. Kennedy*

The man who fears no truth has nothing to fear from a lie.

*Thomas Jefferson*

Life is not comprised entirely of making a living or of arguing about the future or defaming the past. It is the break of the waves in the sun, the contemplation of the eternal fowl of the stream, the stretch of forest and mountain in their manifestation of the Maker—it is all these that soothe our troubles, shame our wickedness, and inspire us to esteem our fellow men—especially other fishermen.

*Herbert Hoover*

We have more will than wallet, but will is what we need.

*George Bush*

I hate deception, even where the imagination only is concerned.

*George Washington*

Every great man of business has a touch of idealist in him somewhere.

*Woodrow Wilson*

I just knew in my heart that it was not right for Dick Nixon to ever be President of this country.

*Lyndon B. Johnson*

---

Unmerited abuse wounds, while unmerited praise has not the power to heal.

*Thomas Jefferson*

---

I had a lifelong ambition to be a professional baseball player, but nobody would sign me.

*Gerald Ford*

---

Things don't turn up in this world until somebody turns them up.

*James A. Garfield*

---

Never spend money before you have it.

*Thomas Jefferson*

---

The price of doing the same old thing is far higher than the price of change.

*Bill Clinton*

Never underestimate a man who overestimates himself.
*Franklin D. Roosevelt*

Those who retire without some occupation can spend their time only in talking about their ills and pills.
*Herbert Hoover*

# Index

**Jim McMullan** is a presidential trivia hobbyist. He has written several books, including *Actors as Artists, Musicians as Artists, This Face You Got, Instant Zen* and *Cheatin' Hearts, Broken Dreams & Stomped on Love*. As an actor, he has starred in dozens of feature films including "Shenandoah," "Downhill Racer," "The Incredible Shrinking Woman," the "The Assassination," and in more than 150 TV shows, including the role of Senator Dowling on "Dallas."